His name is

PATRICK DAWLISH

He is a very large man, with vast
shoulders that his well cut suit cannot
conceal. But for the broken nose, a
legacy of an early battle in the boxing
ring, he would be as handsome as he is
massive . . .
He is always jumping in with both feet
where the police fear to tread. And no
thief, blackmailer or murderer ever comes
up against a tougher, more resourceful,
deadlier enemy than
PATRICK DAWLISH

DON'T LET HIM KILL, one of the
Patrick Dawlish series, is by John
Creasey writing as Gordon Ashe, of
which there are now over forty titles and
many have been published by Corgi
Books.
Born in 1908, John Creasey died in June
1973. Overall, his books have sold nearly
a hundred million copies and have been
translated into 28 languages.
As well as travelling extensively, he had a
particular interest in politics and was the
founder of *All Party Alliance*, which
advocates a new system of government
by the best candidates from all parties
and independents. He fought in five
parliamentary by-elections for the
movement.

Also by John Creasey

and published by CORGI BOOKS

# Don't Let Him Kill

## John Creasey
writing as
## Gordon Ashe

**CORGI BOOKS**
A DIVISION OF TRANSWORLD PUBLISHERS LTD

# DON'T LET HIM KILL

A CORGI BOOK 0 552 09605 9

Originally published in Great Britain
by John Long Ltd.

PRINTING HISTORY
John Long edition published 1960
Corgi edition published 1962
Corgi edition reissued 1974

This book is set in 10 pt Times

Corgi Books are published by Transworld
Publishers Ltd.,
Cavendish House, 57–59 Uxbridge Road,
Ealing, London W.5.
Made and printed in Great Britain by
Cox & Wyman Ltd., London, Reading and Fakenham

# CONTENTS

## CHAPTER I

# WARNINGS

'ARE you sure he's out?' asked Dawlish.

'Quite sure,' answered Superintendent Trivett of New Scotland Yard. 'Be very careful, Pat.'

Dawlish did not respond to that quiet warning, but his strong right hand closed more tightly round the telephone. Outside, the winter sunshine sparkled on frost so white that it looked like snow, covering the close-cut lawns on either side of the drive, the shrubs, the bare branches of the trees which were as stark as if they had been drawn by a master artist on the pale, metallic blue of the sky.

Above his head, a vacuum-cleaner droned as Felicity, Dawlish's wife, pushed it about their bedroom carpet.

'Did you hear me?' Trivett demanded.

'Yes,' answered Dawlish, quietly, 'Yes, I'll be careful, Bill. Gorman meant what he said. I thought I had another three months, though. I'd been wondering whether I could persuade Felicity to go to Cannes for a few weeks, so that I could deal with him myself, but if he was released today I'll never get her away in time.' As if to himself, he added: 'It's bound to be in the newspapers. I hope no lunatic in Fleet Street digs up Gorman's threat against me.'

'Someone is bound to,' Trivett said.

Again Dawlish did not answer. He stood there, tall, massive, flaxen-haired, the sun reflecting on his cornflower blue eyes. His left hand strayed to his face, his forefinger stroked the nose which had been broken, many years ago.

The vacuum droning stopped.

'I shall have him watched for a few weeks.' Trivett said, 'and if he looks like making trouble, I'll try to smack him down. But it's no use fooling ourselves, Pat. Gorman can be deadly, and I doubt whether the fear of being hanged for killing you will put him off. Of course,' the Yard man added in a voice laden with false brightness, 'seven years on the Moor might have changed him; very few men want to go back.'

'Nice thought,' Dawlish remarked, and there was no brightness in his voice. He listened intently for any indication that Felicity was coming downstairs, but the vacuum started up again. 'Bill, thanks for telling me so quickly. If anything happens to make me think he's started, I'll let you know.'

'That's what I was coming to,' Trivett said, all attempt at cheerfulness gone. 'Don't try to handle this on your own, and don't forget that he'll probably try to frighten you and Felicity before doing anything else.'

'I won't forget,' Dawlish assured him. 'Right, Bill. Thanks again.'

He rang off on Trivett's 'Goodbye'. He stood with his arms by his sides, elbows slightly bent, staring at the white-quilted meadowland beyond the road which led here, but he did not really see it. His eyes were shadowed as his thoughts carried him back nearly seven years, to the day when Gorman had said that he would kill the man who had brought him to the dock. Undoubtedly, Gorman had meant exactly that. The police and the Press, used to flamboyant threats made by men in the heat of fury, had also known how serious this one was; there was nothing flamboyant about Gorman.

Felicity had known that, too.

All Dawlish's inclination was to keep this news away from her. He did not want to frighten her, and there was no doubt that this would. They had been quiet, peaceful and happy during the last six months, in some ways the most contented Dawlish had known. There had been a good fruit harvest, the winter had been mild so far and there had been no shadows cast by Dawlish's past—the past of a man who had spent himself first in work for M.I.5., later in work with the police, and as often for the sake of some hapless victim of circumstances.

Whether he wanted to or not, he would have to tell Felicity, not only because there was bound to be a story in one of the newspapers, but because her danger would be at least as great as his. In some ways it would be more urgent and immediate, for Gorman would like nothing better than to make Dawlish suffer through his wife.

Dawlish turned—and the telephone bell rang. He hesitated, staring at its black shape. This might be a call from the village, from a friend, from someone who wanted to know if he had any of his fine crop of Newtown pippins left. It rang again and again, and soon the maid would come hustling from the kitchen to answer it, or else Felicity would lift up the extension in the bedroom.

He picked up the receiver.

'Is that Alum 1434?' a girl asked.

'Yes.'

'I've a personal call from London for a Mr. Patrick Dawlish.'

'I am Dawlish,' Dawlish said. He was still acutely sensitive to sounds upstairs, and when the vacuum stopped again he glanced at the ceiling. Noises on the line were followed by a woman's voice, then by a man's.

'Mr. Dawlish?'

'Yes.'

'Mr. Dawlish, my name is Hedford, of the *Daily Globe*. I wonder if you will be good enough——'

'Hold on a minute,' Dawlish said. He put the receiver on the table, and listened intently to the movements upstairs. It was possible that Felicity had lifted the extension and was listening in; and he did not want her to find out about Gorman by chance. He heard her walking across the room, away from the bedside and the telephone. He picked up the instrument, and said stonily, 'Yes, Mr. Hedford?'

'I wonder if you will be good enough to give me a little information about your activities against a man named Gorman—Maurice Gorman,' Hedford said briskly. 'I don't know whether you are aware that he was released from Dartmoor early this morning, after earning an extra three months' remission for saving the life of a warder two months ago.'

'Yes, I'd heard,' said Dawlish. 'I wonder if you would like to earn three months' remission for my wife, too.'

There was a startled pause.

'What did you say?' Hedford was rather a precise speaker, who pronounced each word with great clarity.

'Gorman threatened to kill me,' Dawlish went on quietly, 'and at the time he probably meant it. Seven years of breaking stones may have softened his resolve, so probably there's nothing to worry about. If there isn't, then there's no need for my wife to be worried by newspaper stories. The less said about this matter at this stage the better.'

'I do understand your point of view,' said Hedford, earnestly, and he might as well have declared briskly that nothing would stop him from using this story. 'But if we don't use it, Mr. Dawlish, other newspapers are bound to, and not all of them will have the courtesy to call you. As a matter of fact you've given me a new slant. I might be able to use the story to mutual advantage. May I say that in your considered opinion Gorman will not carry out his threat?'

'No,' answered Dawlish, brusquely. There was no point in irritating a newspaperman; that never paid; on the other hand he was goaded by that burning fear for Felicity. He needed time to think, time to manoeuvre, and this shock had come with cruel unexpectedness. 'No,' he repeated, less sharply, 'I don't want to be quoted at all, Mr. Hedford.'

'So you *are* alarmed,' the newspaperman observed.

After a moment's pause, Dawlish chuckled, and although it took considerable effort, he managed to sound natural.

'I can't stop you from putting words in my mouth,' he said, 'but there aren't many people who will believe you if you take that line. Very few would believe that I would admit to being alarmed even if I were. I'm quite sure my wife will be scared, and I'd like to prevent it, but you must do whatever your editor and your conscience will let you.'

'Mr. Dawlish,' Hedford said, still earnestly and now with a note of reproach in his voice, 'this isn't a matter of conscience, you know. My job is to report news—*facts*—to the readers of the *Globe*.' How portentous could a newspaperman be, Dawlish wondered, and why did he have to be tackled by this one? 'Will you at least confirm that I have the *facts* right.'

'If you have, yes,' answered Dawlish. 'But have you.'

He heard Felicity coming down the stairs, so he turned away from the door, looking out of the window again, trying to make sure that she didn't come in; if she saw his face, she almost certainly would.

'Thank you,' Hedford said, with a touch of irony. 'The facts as I understand them, are that Maurice Gorman and his son, then a youth of nineteen, were involved together in an attempt to swindle an elderly woman out of a fortune variously estimated at between one hundred and two hundred thousand pounds. Her name was Vaze—Mrs. Emily Vaze, who lived at Wimbledon. A friend of Mrs. Vaze told you that she was worried about Gorman's influence on Mrs. Vaze, and as a result you made some investigations, and discovered that he had a prison record for the same kind of confidence trick—he had undertaken to invest Mrs. Vaze's money.'

The precisely uttered words went on and on. Felicity reached the foot of the stairs, and Dawlish could hear her approach this room, her footsteps softened by the carpet. He guessed that she was at the doorway.

'Am I right so far?' inquired Hedford.

'Yes, quite right,' answered Dawlish, and tried to make his voice sound casual.

'Thank you. You first dealt with Gorman's son, believing that it would be easier to break him down than to make his

10

father admit what he was doing. You were quite right. The son—named Maximilian—confessed, so that you were able to warn Mrs. Vaze, and also lodge certain information with the police. Maximilian Gorman attempted to escape from you, so that he could warn his father, thus giving his father an opportunity to leave England for France. You gave chase, and in the chase the youth attempted to climb over a railway embankment, slipped, fell and broke his neck.'

'Very well summed up,' conceded Dawlish.

He could not be sure whether Felicity was in the doorway, looking at him, or whether she had gone into the kitchen and was talking to the maid. That more than anything else troubled him.

'Thank you,' Hedford said, with satisfaction. 'Tell me this: at the time that Gorman threatened to kill you, when he was in the dock, did you take him seriously?'

'I always take that kind of thing seriously,' Dawlish replied.

'Do you indeed? I can certainly understand it. Mr. Dawlish, on reflection, do you think that you could make any statement for the *Globe*? I am sure that it could be used to your advantage rather than your disadvantage.'

'You're very kind,' Dawlish said formally, 'but no'.

'If at any time you should change your mind I hope you will get in touch with me,' said Hedford obligingly. 'One other thing—is it true to say that you have retired from active participation in—ah—investigations of the same nature?'

'Yes.'

'And that you have a small fruit farm in a village near Haslemere?'

'I also keep pigs,' announced Dawlish.

'Do you indeed? That is very interesting. Thank you very much for being so frank with me, Mr. Dawlish. Goodbye.'

'Goodbye,' said Dawlish and put the receiver down slowly, but did not immediately turn round. If Felicity were there, this was as good a time to break the news to her as any. He turned his head.

There she stood.

From their early days together there had been a kind of telepathy between them. No one could ever be as quick as Felicity in sensing Dawlish's mood, in realizing when there was something wrong. Bad news must have sounded in his tone of voice, or else shown in the way he had stood with his

11

back to her; or perhaps it showed now in his expression, although he gave her a broad grin.

She did not smile back.

She was tall, still slender, high-breasted, with slim, beautiful legs. She had hair which was neither dark nor fair, never really untidy, never looking as if she had come fresh from a hairdresser. She had wide-set grey-green eyes, and a very fair, fresh complexion. She was not beautiful by accepted standards, but attractive by all. She was lovely in Dawlish's eyes, she always would be, and she had never been lovelier than she was now.

'What is it, Pat?' she asked, coming forward. 'You've had two London calls, haven't you? Don't say that someone wants you to start playing policeman again; I really couldn't stand it.' When Dawlish didn't answer, but put his head on one side as if to start arguing, the telephone rang for the third time within half an hour; and for the second time it made him jump. He saw Felicity frown, wished that he had kept better control of his nerves, but was glad of a little respite, for Felicity must be told the truth very carefully indeed. He plucked up the receiver and tried to infuse a kind of gaiety into his voice as he said:

'Pat Dawlish here!'

'Is that Mr. Dawlish of Alum 1434?'

'Yes,' Dawlish answered, and thought, 'Here's another newspaperman, blast them all,' He held on, twisting round so that he could see Felicity, as the operator said:

'Hold on, please, Mr. Dawlish, I have a personal call for you from Exeter.'

'Exeter?' Dawlish echoed, and looked as startled as he sounded.

The girl had gone off the line, and did not answer. Felicity moved forward, while Dawlish tried to absorb the implications of this call.

Gorman could have reached Exeter, by now, on his way to London from Dartmoor.

CHAPTER II

THREATS

FELICITY reached Dawlish's side before the call came through, touched the back of his hand clutching the telephone, and asked in a subdued voice:

'What is it, Pat?'

He pulled a face at her.

'Not quite what you think,' he assured her. 'It will probably fizzle out.' He wished that he could put more conviction into his voice, for he saw that she was a long way from reassured. Then he heard the woman speak again.

'Are you still there, Mr. Dawlish?'

'Yes.'

'Here is your call from Exeter,' the operator enthused, and there was a click, a little murmuring sound on the line, and—silence.

'Hallo,' said Dawlish, and winked at his wife.

The line was silent except for mumbling and buzzing. Dawlish felt his fingers tighten round the receiver, and felt himself sweating; his forehead and the back of his neck were cold in the draught from an open window. Felicity repeated '*What is it?*' more urgently, and this time there was no point in trying to reassure her.

'I'll tell you in a minute, sweet,' Dawlish whispered, and as he finished, a man's voice sounded in his ear, but he did not catch what was said.

'Hallo? Who is that?' he asked.

'I am speaking for a friend of yours, recently from Dartmoor,' a man answered, in a slightly husky voice; the kind of voice which might be heard if he were speaking through gauze held over the mouthpiece of the telephone. 'He asked me to give you his regards, and he especially asked me to give his love to Mrs. Dawlish.'

Dawlish found himself wanting to shout '*Who are you?*' He felt the tension at his fingers because of the tightness of his grip. He saw real anxiety appear on Felicity's face because of his behaviour. He made himself speak very calmly as he asked:

'Are you speaking for Maurice Gorman?'

'What an interesting idea!' the man explained, and there was a note of laughter in the way he said it. 'I wonder who put that into your mind? The police, perhaps? Yes, Mr. Dawlish. I am speaking for Gorman. I don't know whether you know him as well as I do, but I've known him all of his life, and there is one characteristic of his which everyone ought to know: he is a man of his word.'

Dawlish said: 'I can believe it. Will you give him a message for me?'

There was no immediate answer, and although he was

eager for the speaker's next words, he had a moment to study Felicity. He saw the way she bit her upper lip, and could tell from her expression that the name Gorman had conveyed a great deal to her, all unpleasant. She moved back a pace and sat on the window-seat.

The man from Exeter said: 'Yes, I will give him a message. What is it?'

'Every now and again there comes a time when it's better for a man to break his word rather than keep it.' Dawlish answered. 'This is one of those occasions. Tell Gorman that I would like to talk to him about it.'

'You would? How *very* interesting.' The hint of laughter seemed even stronger; rollicking. 'I will certainly tell him. You and your wife may expect to hear from him at any time —day and night, Mr. Dawlish, at home or away, in sickness and in health, week in, week out. Good morning!'

He rang off.

Dawlish put down the receiver, and took out a handkerchief and wiped the back of his neck and then his forehead. He stood looking down at Felicity, who leaned against a window, her eyes at their roundest, clearest and most direct. Dawlish moved back and sat on the arm of a chair, before saying:

'Sorry, sweet.'

'I thought he would be in prison until after Easter,' Felicity said carefully.

'So you hadn't forgotten him?'

'I've forgotten a lot of threats, but not that one,' Felicity said. 'I remember it far too vividly. The trouble was——'

She didn't finish.

'The son,' Dawlish said.

'Pat, it isn't reasonable to blame you for it!' exclaimed Felicity, getting up. 'The father taught the son everything, and led him on. It was Gorman's fault entirely, it wasn't yours at all. It's a wicked thing.'

'Yes,' Dawlish agreed, bleakly. 'No doubt about that.'

'There's no sense in it!'

'But there's some danger in it,' Dawlish pointed out, and for the first time since any of the calls had come through he gave a really spontaneous grin. 'As if you didn't know! Sweet, we're up against something more complicated than a bad man who apprenticed his son to his own crooked way of living. Gorman is a much stronger than average personality anyhow, and the son's death a fixation. Everything I've ever heard from people who've seen him in Dartmoor proves

14

that.' He smiled again, less brightly, and was relieved that he was feeling more himself; he could almost forget how sharply the calls had shaken him. 'I've talked to three convicts who worked with him on the Moor, and they've all said the same thing: all Gorman dreams about is getting out and getting his revenge. No use blinking at it, Fel.'

After a long pause, Felicity said: 'No, I suppose not. What—what did he say on the telephone?'

'I'm not even sure that it was Gorman,' Dawlish answered, then told her what Trivett had said, about the call from the *Globe*, and the third call, from this 'friend' of Gorman. Felicity took all this with outward calm, and when he had finished, she asked:

'Why did you suggest seeing him?'

Dawlish wiped the back of his neck again, stood up and stepped to the window. The sun seemed to be more brilliant than ever, and near it the sky was more white than blue. A small car flashed by the end of the drive gates, going much too fast. Dawlish could make out the spikes of shooting daffodils in those parts of the grassy banks of the drive where they flourished spring after spring; this year they promised so well.

What the hell was the matter with him? Gorman was only one man, and there was the whole weight of the police against him, as well as his, Dawlish's; and plenty of others would jump at the chance of helping. What was there in Gorman which could affect him like this?

At heart, he knew; a steely purpose and burning hatred. Add the two together, and it could be the most deadly thing in the world.

'Why did you?' Felicity asked, patiently.

'I don't really know, Fel, except that I thought it would be a good thing to size him up as soon as possible. It's always better to know the man you're up against than to fight in the dark. He's bound to be different in some ways. He might have a weakness, too. He was believed to be broke when he went down, which means that he probably hasn't any money now. He isn't likely to have many friends, in spite of the man who called from Exeter.'

Dawlish paused, and frowned, taken by a new thought, and Felicity did not interrupt.

'Fel,' he went on abruptly, 'we've got to play this to win. There are two ways to start. Either you've got to be out of the country, quite safe from him until it's over—that way I'll be able to concentrate more. Or else we've got to do every-

15

thing together, with you knowing every move, every likely trick, everything in my mind. Don't say that *of course* you're going to stay. What you want to do or what I want to do doesn't matter a damn. The only thing that matters is to beat Gorman. Let's talk about it later, when we've had time to think. I just said that he isn't likely to have many friends, but unless that was Gorman disguising his voice, he's using at least one man who knows all about his threat and his plans. There may be others,'

Felicity asked, sharply, 'What do you mean?'

'Fel, Gorman is not the only man I've helped to send to Dartmoor,' Dawlish answered very carefully. 'Two years ago there were seven men on the Moor and five others in different parts of the country. Not all of them would take a hand in a vendetta, but two or three might hate me enough to try.'

He saw the colour ebb slowly from Felicity's cheeks.

'You mean he may have planned it with others before they left Dartmoor?'

'It's possible, yes.'

After a pause, Felicity said in a firm voice: 'Yes, of course it is. The first thing you have to do, darling, is find out who might work with him. Bill Trivett will help there, won't he?'

'Oh, yes,' said Dawlish. 'He'll get the names of all Dawlish-haters whom Gorman might know, and get their movements checked. Bill won't miss a trick. And we mustn't miss a trick, either,' he added, in a lighter, brighter tone. 'I prepared a comprehensive dossier on Gorman, and what I missed the Yard gave me—they were always worried about him. I'll check Gorman's relations, his pre-Dartmoor friends, and whether he's got any money. I should say that our biggest chance is finding him on his beam ends. He might soften up if he thinks it would be worth while.'

Felicity made no comment. Dawlish recognized the stubborn look in her eyes, and found himself smiling again as he asked:

'Don't you agree, sweet?'

'If you're thinking that you might be able to head Gorman off by bribing him, no, I don't agree,' she answered. 'If you were to offer him money, he would probably take it, and use it against you. I don't disagree about seeing him, but it will probably be a waste of time trying to talk him out of anything. You won't talk me out of anything, either,' she added, very firmly. 'It will certainly be a waste of time talking things over. I shall stay with you.' Quite suddenly, she laughed at

Dawlish, and went on in a lighter tone: 'Bless you, precious, but I'm *not* blind or dumb! Every time you've talked about me having a month in France just after Easter, I've known perfectly well that you wanted me out of the way when Gorman was released. Nothing would have made me go.'

'You little devil,' Dawlish said, and moved so swiftly that she couldn't dodge him. 'I always wondered why you kept hedging. Last year you were only too ready to jump at the chance.' He held her close enough to feel the beating of her heart, even though she strained her head back to look into his eyes. 'Fel,' he said, 'I couldn't take it if anything happened to you. It would be——'

She interrupted very quickly:

'It's no use, Pat, I won't go. Don't start fighting me as well as Gorman, he's quite enough for the two of us.' When he didn't answer, she closed her eyes, and Dawlish held her so closely that his great arms seemed to crush her.

At last he let her go.

'All right,' he said, gruffly. 'Have it your own way.'

They were still standing close when the telephone bell rang again. This time Dawlish deliberately let it go on for half a minute before releasing Felicity and stretching out for the receiver.

He was beginning to realize how much of his anxiety had been for and about Felicity. At the moment he felt that he hadn't a care in the world, the threat from Maurice Gorman seemed almost trivial.

He clapped his hand over the mouthpiece, thrust it towards Felicity, and said:

'If it's another newspaper tell them I'm out.'

Felicity took the receiver, and spoke as if she hadn't a serious thought in the world.

'This is Alum 1434.' She paused, and Dawlish saw her face light up and knew that this couldn't be bad news. 'It's Ted!' she flashed at him, and listened again while Dawlish could just make out the voice of Ted Beresford, close friend of the family. He was rejoicing in Felicity's pleasure, and felt a kind of exhilaration in preparing for battle. Ted had helped him against Gorman. But for Ted . . .

Dawlish saw Felicity's expression change to one of alarm, and she cried, 'Oh, no!'

All Dawlish's tension flooded back. It was difficult not to stretch out and take the telephone from her, but there was no

17

need for that. Felicity lowered it against her breast, hesitated, and looked far more distressed than before.

'Joan's missing,' she said abruptly. 'Ted sounds frantic.'

'Frantic' was exactly how Dawlish would feel if anything happened to his wife.

## CHAPTER III

## ACTION

THERE was tautness in Ted Beresford's deep voice, and Dawlish knew exactly what Felicity had meant. He himself just said, 'What's it all about, Ted?' and the answer came swift and alarmed.

'She's been away for a few days, in Oxford with her mother. She was coming back last night, but I wasn't too surprised when she didn't turn up. I didn't realize that my telephone was out of order until I had a call at the garage across the mews this morning—twenty minutes ago, that's all—and I realized there was something wrong. A man asked me if I'd realized that Joan was missing. The words he actually used were "your wife is missing". I called her mother's place right away, of course, and Joan left on the two-fifteen bus yesterday afternoon. She should have been at Paddington a little after six.'

Beresford stopped speaking.

Dawlish said, 'This man who telephoned, Ted—what was his voice like?'

'I'd like to cut his throat,' answered Beresford savagely. 'The swine was talking as if he could burst himself with laughing.'

'And was his voice husky and a little distorted?'

'What's this?' Beresford exclaimed. 'What do you know about the devil?'

There was no point in keeping anything from Beresford; Dawlish would have preferred to be with him, face to face, but could not wait that long. The easing of his own tension was quite familiar; tension was born of threat, easement out of action, or the need for it.

'For God's sake say something!' Beresford exploded.

'Yes,' promised Dawlish, very quietly. 'I know how you feel, Ted. I had a telephone call from the same man, soon after you did. He reminded me that Maurice Gorman was released from Dartmoor early this morning.'

After a pause, Beresford said in a hoarse voice, '*My God.*'

There was a long silence, and in it Dawlish could imagine the expression on his friend's face, could actually hear the way Beresford began to draw in deep breaths, as the shock caught up with him. Then: 'I'm going to telephone the Oxford Police from this 'phone, and ask them to start making inquiries at Oxford Railway Station. Will you call Bill Trivett?' Beresford had never been a man to waste words, and in times of crisis had always found emotion difficult to express or show.

'Yes,' Dawlish said. 'And I'll have him get the G.P.O. busy on your telephone.'

'Thanks, I'll call you again in twenty minutes.'

'I'll be here,' promised Dawlish. He put the receiver down, acutely aware of Felicity's intense gaze, and rubbed the broken bridge of his nose again. His throat felt tight. 'I'm going to get Bill Trivett busy from the London end,' he told her, and lifted the receiver and dialled Trunks. As he listened to the ringing sound, he looked at Felicity, and began to speak. 'From this moment on, don't take the slightest chance. Don't go out into the garden without someone else. Get the shopkeepers to deliver what you want, don't go and fetch anything until we've checked the neighbourhood. Don't answer the front or the back door on your own.' His low-pitched voice made the warnings seem more frightening.

'All right,' Felicity said.

'Number please,' said the operator, and Dawlish gave Whitehall 1212, looking at Felicity, but for once seeing someone in her place; seeing Joan Beresford, a happy, contented, warmhearted woman who had built her life on a belief in goodness.

\* \* \* \* \*

The previous afternoon Joan Beresford had waited for ten minutes for the bus to take her to Oxford Station, scorning a taxi because she had plenty of time. Her mother, who shared a cottage with another elderly woman, had looked quite young and attractive as she stood by the gate of the cottage, waving as the bus moved off.

It would be half an hour before the bus reached Oxford, Joan knew; half an hour in which to sit back and relax, to forget the little tensions between young and old, and remember the pleasures of the visit more than its tedium, smiling at the thought that she would be home for dinner tonight. They were in the middle of a good spell of weather, the sun struck warm through the window, and the bus was going to the station terminus, so it would not greatly matter if she dozed off.

She did this journey several times a year, it was almost literally true that she could do it in her sleep.

She found herself thinking about Ted, and how he would be managing at the flat with the help of the daily woman. He had probably enjoyed fiddling about on his own, Joan reflected, and he had certainly been busy. He lived in what was politely called semi-retirement, which meant that he attended a number of board meetings of small companies once every month, and occasionally did a little top-level selling for a company which manufactured paper, and another which dealt in plastics. He spent much more time on some charitable committee or other, being driven by a conscience which never seemed assuaged. There would be so much to talk about that they would probably be at it until midnight.

She dozed. . . .

She dozed in the train from Oxford to Paddington, too, but as always, London stimulated her. She went to telephone Ted, who would fetch her. She got no reply, and the telephone made queer noises before the operator told her that it was out of order. That would please Ted! It was the tail-end of the rush-hour, she couldn't get a taxi, and did not get a seat on the bus from Paddington to Hyde Park Corner. By then it was dark, but London was lit by a myriad lights, all of them seeming to converge at the corner as the traffic surged about it. She got off the bus at twenty past six, and decided not to worry about a taxi. It was only a ten minutes' walk to the mews flat, even if the case was heavy.

When she was half-way home she wished she had been more persistent in waiting for a taxi, but it wasn't worth while now. She turned off Park Lane and into the warren of streets which made up Mayfair, and was within sight of the entrance to the mews where she lived, when a man stepped out of a doorway just in front of her. His appearance was so startling and unexpected that it made her jump. She noticed without thinking, that a car was drawn up outside the house.

'Sorry, miss,' the man said in a hard, metallic sounding voice. 'I can't do anything right this evening.'

Joan could hardly have cared less.

'I wonder if you know where this address is,' the man went on, and took a slip of paper out of his pocket. As Joan put her case down and looked at the paper, he took it nearer the car. 'You'll see better here,' he said, but that wasn't true until he opened the rear door of the car, and the courtesy light went on. She had a strange impression: that he was crowding her.

20

'Ah, that's better,' he said, and smoothed the piece of paper down with his thumb as he thrust it towards her. To see what was on it, she had to lower her head, and she was vaguely annoyed with the man's manner and the fuss he was making.

With awful suddenness, annoyance faded into terror.

The man let the slip of paper fall, and his hand clutched her throat, almost throttling her, and making it impossible for her to cry out. She did not see another man squatting inside the back of the car, who stretched forward and took her shoulders and lugged her towards him. The pressure at her throat increased, thumb and fingers seemed to be digging into the flesh, the pressure at her neck and now at her lungs was agonizing.

She could not breathe.

She was just aware of being hoisted on to the back seat of the car, of sound and of movement, and the sharp hoot of a car horn. Then, worse terror came. The man shifted his position. Both hands were round her neck, both thumbs were burying themselves into her throat, her breast was heaving, the awful constriction at the back of her throat, at her ears and at her lungs seemed to become a crushing weight.

There was blackness all about her, and a rushing sound in her ears, as if she was screaming at herself in her great terror. Her last conscious thought seemed to scream inside her mind.

*'They're killing me—they're killing me!'*

* * * * *

Dawlish heard Felicity walking about upstairs again, getting ready to leave for London; they had to hurry to Ted. Felicity would be ready in twenty minutes, with enough things packed for a night or two in London. Trivett's line had been engaged for five minutes, but now his call was coming through. Dawlish was standing by the window; he felt as if he had been on the telephone all the morning. He could not bring himself to relax, and fear for Joan Beresford heightened his fear for Felicity. He scanned the near and distant countryside, half afraid that someone out there was watching this house, and his mind was racing over the things which had to be done, and done quickly.

Trivett came on the line.

'Yes, Pat?'

'It looks as if Gorman's started,' Dawlish said quietly, 'and it looks as if he's using someone else, Bill.' He told Trivett exactly what had happened, knowing that Trivett

21

would feel almost as badly as he did himself. Then he said, 'Mind making a few notes of what I think would help?'

'I'm ready.'

'Thanks,' said Dawlish. 'Ted's talking to the Oxford Police now. Joan should have reached Paddington a little before six o'clock yesterday evening, so if you can find out whether she got there, it would help. Then, we ought to know how near she got to the mews. It's pretty obvious that Ted's telephone was tampered with, to make sure that Joan couldn't telephone him to fetch her, as she usually does. If she was kidnapped, it would probably be from near her home, the one place assailants would be sure of finding her.' He paused for a moment, still staring out of the window, and unexpectedly he saw a man appear at the open drive gates. He could not see him clearly, but was almost certain that it was a tramp. He watched as the man stared at the house, read the name on the gates—Four Ways, because this was close to the road junction approaching Alum Village—and started moving towards the house.

It was a tramp; elderly, grey-haired and incredibly ragged.

'Yes, Pat,' Trivett went on.

'Ted's telephone is out of order and he got a message at the garage in the mews, so someone has studied the situation closely. Can you whistle the G.P.O. to check Ted's telephone quickly?'

'Yes,' Trivett answered. 'What did you mean when you said that Gorman might be using someone else?'

The tramp was much nearer, walking steadily up the steep drive. His hair was a frizzy grey mop, and where the sun caught his lean, sallow features there showed a week-old stubble, spiky and grey, and growing high on ruddy cheeks. He wore at least three big overcoats, the top one buttoned tightly, so that although his face and legs were thin he was bulging at the belly. The only new-looking and incongruous thing about him were his shoes, bright, shiny and brown, and obviously much too large for him. If he saw Dawlish in the window, he took no notice. Dawlish saw him turn away from the front door; tramps would go to the back.

Dawlish said to Trivett: 'Gorman was supposed to be broke, and he didn't work with others, so he wouldn't have many friends. But he might have teamed up with other convicts, and made this a co-operative affair. He was still in Dartmoor Prison last night, so he couldn't have taken any personal part in what happened to Joan.'

'I get it,' Trivett said heavily, and as if he did not like the implications any more than Dawlish did. There was a bleak tone in his voice as he went on: 'I'll check all old lags who might hate your guts. The only visitor Gorman ever had on the Moor was his sister-in-law, but she wasn't involved in the crimes.'

'I remember her,' Dawlish said. 'Bill, I——'

'If you're coming to London, you'd better make sure that the Haselmere Police watch Four Ways,' Trivett interrupted. 'If you leave the house empty, or with only a maid in it, something could be planted while you're away.'

Dawlish gave a tense, taut grin.

'The man who thinks of everything,' he riposted. 'I'll have a word with the local cops. Thanks, Bill. I'll call or look in this afternoon. Just now, there's a chap at the back door I ought to talk to.'

He rang off; and moved.

Dawlish on the move and in a hurry was almost unbelievable. One moment he was putting the telephone down, the next he was striding along the passage to the kitchen. He heard the back door ring, and stood by the closed kitchen door, listening. He thought that Felicity stopped moving about upstairs; she might have heard the bell ringing, too. Ivy, the daily maid from the village, thumped across the kitchen, and a moment later she demanded:

'Now what do you want?'

'Would you spare a crust for a hungry man?' asked the tramp, in a high-pitched voice and a sing-song accent which Dawlish could not place. It might be Welsh; it might also be Scottish. 'It's hungry I am after coming a long way, and a lady of the likes of you wouldn't turn away a hungry man.'

'Oh *wouldn't* I?' asked Ivy.

She would not, Dawlish knew. She had a reputation, and Felicity did nothing to spoil it, for being over-generous with tramps and gypsies. Felicity started to move about again, and Dawlish stepped closer to the door so that he would be at hand if there were any sign of emergency.

'No, I'm sure you wouldn't,' the tramp said to the maid. 'I'd be glad even of a bite of bread and a cup of cold water.'

Less than five minutes later, Dawlish heard the man's warm 'thank ye', heard him move away, heard the back door close. A minute after that he saw the tramp walking down the drive, those shiny brown shoes glinting in the sun. He was eating the hunk of pork pie which Ivy had given him,

23

and carrying two large, red apples in his right hand. He was more brisk, with quite a jaunty swing in his walk, as if he had everything he wanted.

Dawlish said, *sotto voce*, 'If I go on like this I'll be seeing Gorman in everyone who comes,' and hesitated at the doorway of the drawing-room. He could telephone the Haslemere Police, but this wasn't the easiest subject to discuss by telephone, and he could easily call at the police station when he left for London; going via Haslemere would only put ten extra minutes on the journey. He hurried upstairs. Felicity was sitting in front of the dressing-table, putting on lipstick; she was ready but for her hat and coat, and the packed case was on the bed.

'Can I put my brief-case on top of that?' Dawlish asked. 'I'll take the papers from the Gorman file.'

'It will help to keep the clothes in position,' Felicity answered.

'Ta. I won't be three shakes,' Dawlish promised. 'When Ted calls, tell him we'll be at the flat by eleven-thirty or so.'

'All right,' said Felicity. 'What did Bill say?'

'We can count on the Yard for hundred per cent co-operation,' Dawlish assured her. He slipped out of a pair of flannels and an old sports jacket, and began to dress rapidly in a suit, yet could not prevent himself from getting the file of papers and glancing through some of them, to refresh his memory. He was almost ready when the telephone bell rang. Felicity talked to Ted, and for a split second Dawlish stood looking at her, hoping desperately that there was news of Joan. There was none, obviously. Dawlish finished dressing, and Felicity said:

'Ted tried to get Tim but there was no answer.'

'Is Ted trying the club?'

'Yes,' Felicity said, and tried to smile. The second telephone-call from Ted seemed to have upset her more than anything else, as if the fear that Joan was in grave danger had become much sharper. 'For goodness' sake hurry up!'

'Won't be two shakes,' Dawlish said, optimistically. 'Why don't you nip down and get the car out?' He tossed her the keys of his Allard, and she missed them, but they fell on the bed. She picked them up, and hurried out and down the stairs, he heard the passage door to the kitchen open, and there followed a murmur of conversation. Felicity had to tell the maid what to do, of course. The wise thing would be to let her go home until they returned from London. He could make arrangements with the Haselmere Police, though there was no need to tell Ivy now.

He ran a comb through his crisp flaxen hair, wafted hairs off the collar and shoulders, closed the case, picked it up, and swung towards the landing.

He was on the top stair when he heard a great roar of sound. A door banged savagely, the house shook, and he felt the blast of an explosion whining up the stairs.

CHAPTER IV

FRIGHT

THERE was a smell of burning, the frightening echo of the explosion, and there was dread in Dawlish as he raced down the stairs. He dropped the suitcase when he saw that the kitchen door was shut; that was the door which must have slammed. He did not have any conscious thought, but that dread for Felicity.

He snatched at the handle of the door and thrust at it, but it would not budge. He tried again, with the same result. It had been strained at the hinges and was jammed tight. He drew back a yard, and flung his great body forward, shoulder against the door; it gave way and he staggered into a kitchen filled with smoke that was tinged red with flame.

On the floor, close to the dresser, Ivy lay on her face. Broken china made a kind of shroud for her. *A shroud?* The fire was in the garden doorway, and the smoke blotted out the actual doorway itself, as well as the window. There was no sign of Felicity, at least she wasn't in here. But if the explosion had struck her outside she might be even more badly hurt. Dawlish flung himself through the smoke, felt heat singe his right hand, reached the steps which led to the garden—and saw Felicity reeling against an outside wall. Her hat had been blown off, her skirt was rucked up round her waist, she looked as if she had been shaken but was not badly hurt. Dawlish swung back towards the kitchen, reached Ivy and bent over her. He felt her pulse, and it was beating. He did not think that she was badly hurt, any more than Felicity. There was a nasty wound on her right cheek, and some scratches on her forehead and her neck; that seemed all. He ran his hands over her arms and legs, to make sure that nothing was broken, then lifted her and carried her through the smoke and flames and into the garden.

Felicity was standing upright, still dazed, but obviously struggling to regain her self-control.

'Look after Ivy,' Dawlish said hoarsely. 'I've got to get that fire out.' He went down on one knee and put the maid down on the grass at the back of the house, in the full, strong sunlight; before he turned away he saw that her eyes were flickering. Felicity did not say a word, just bent over the woman. Dawlish sprinted to the garage, where there was a fire extinguisher, began to operate it as he came back, and sprayed the flames at once. A hiss of smoke came, followed by a lathery mass from the extinguisher which put the flames out, and soon the whole of the doorway looked like a mammoth bubble bath. The smell of the extinguisher foam and the stench of burning wood and rubber were revolting.

Dawlish finished, put the extinguisher down, and wiped his forehead with the back of his hand.

'It must have been that tramp,' Felicity said, unsteadily. Dawlish turned round to see her close by him. Behind her, Ivy was sitting up on a garden seat, conscious but dazed. 'Ivy's all right, but she ought to see a doctor,' Felicity went on.

'Yes,' Dawlish said, 'Get the car out, and I'll——'

He broke off, as if startled, and looked towards the brick-built garage at one side of the house, some distance from it. 'No, I'll get the car out,' he decided. 'You call the police and they'll fix the doctor. The quicker we find out what started the fire——'

'It *must* have been that tramp.' Felicity still sounded dazed.

'Could have been,' Dawlish agreed. 'Probably was, too, but someone else might have come by stealth and left the little *billet doux*. Won't be long.' He made himself leave her, although frightened that there was danger to her every moment. He opened the sliding doors of the garage, and looked at the Allard and at Felicity's little Sunbeam. He studied the floor and the bonnets of the cars and saw no sign of finger-prints, then looked inside, checked there was nothing wrong at the controls, and pushed up the bonnets of each car in turn. He made sure that nothing was connected to the self-starters, that no explosive had been put in either of them.

He put a piece of old sacking down on the ground under-neath the large car, went down, and wriggled so that he could look up into the gaping bowels of the car, all dark and dirty from oil and the road. He studied the chassis, the exhaust, the suspension, the petrol tank, the oil filter, the springs, before he saw what he had been looking for, the thing which increased his dread of what might happen soon.

Fastened to the inside of the offside wheel was a small grey packet, rather like a hair shampoo sachet, but made of some rubbery substance. It was fastened by wire twisted round a nut. He hitched himself into a better position for handling it, then began to untwist the wire. He did not hesitate to do that, although he felt sure that this container would explode when subjected to sudden pressure or to a jerky movement, the kind of movement inevitable if the car went over a hole in the road, or bumped more than usual. He did not know how long it took, but at last he had the rubber container safely in his left hand. He placed it on the garage floor with extreme care, well away from the car, then wriggled out in the other direction. He brushed himself down, took the wheel and put the key in the ignition. He hesitated for a moment, holding his breath in case he had missed some other booby-trap.

He turned the key and stabbed the self-starter.

The engine fired at the first touch, then gave a sharp backfire. Dawlish gritted his teeth. The engine started, and he eased off the brakes and took the car out of the garage. He sat at the wheel for a long moment, wiping his forehead again, and realized that he was clenching his teeth so hard that they hurt.

Ahead of him was the brightness and beauty, the quiet and serenity, of the Surrey countryside.

He heard a car engine coming from the direction of Alum Village, only a little more than a mile away. The engine was changing gear. He knew the exact spot, the corner coming out of the village; it sounded as if someone was in a hurry. He got out of the car, went back to the garage and stared down at the sachet, then picked up a wooden box and placed it over it. He still felt hot, and was sweating freely. He heard the whine of the approaching car engine, and stood in front of the garage, watching the dark top of a car racing along the road. His whole body was tense, lest this should be another visitation from Gorman or the 'friends' of Gorman.

The car slowed down; so it was coming here. It turned into the drive, and he saw the word '*Police*' on the front. He relaxed, realizing that the police must have started out within a minute or two of getting Felicity's call. The fire department would soon be here, too. He glanced at the protective wooden box, then went round to the back of the house. Ivy sat very still, with Felicity bending over her, bathing the wound in her cheek, and the scratches. Ivy was saying in a

27

shrill voice what a terrible thing it had been, if she hadn't been standing with her back to the door it would have killed her. The more garrulous she was, the less serious her injuries, Dawlish persuaded himself.

'The police are here and we'll soon have you looked after properly,' he said to the maid, and added jerkily to Felicity: 'I can fix things with the police here, we won't have to lose time going to Haslemere.' He stepped over the blackened doorsteps, and for the first time realized just how much damage had been done in the kitchen. There was hardly a whole plate or cup left on the dresser, it looked as if a whirlwind had wrecked the place. Cabinet doors were hanging loosely on their hinges, saucepans were piled up in a heap in one corner, the rubbish bin had been upset and the garbage strewn all over the floor near the sink.

He heard the police car draw up outside.

\* \* \* \* \*

It took Dawlish twenty minutes to explain what had happended, urge the police to treat the sachet with extreme care, arrange for Ivy to be taken to Haslemere Hospital, and to make arrangements for the house to be watched. All the time he found himself thinking bitterly that it was the old story of locking the stable door after the horse had gone.

What other devilry had been planned?

How long had this been going on?

How many people were working with Gorman?

Could he hope to prove that Gorman was in fact responsible?

The thoughts churned over and over in his mind as he drove towards London. Felicity said very little, and whenever he glanced at her she was staring straight ahead. She was badly frightened, of course; she saw the possibilities as clearly as he did, and knew that neither of them could be sure what would happen at any moment of the day or night.

Was that exaggerating the situation? Dawlish asked himself. Wasn't it really playing into Gorman's hands, because it was so obvious that Gorman was deliberately setting out to terrorize him?

He kept picturing the jaunty attitude of the tramp as the man had walked down the drive. At the time it had looked as if he had been thoroughly content with the food and drink and the half-crown which Ivy had undoubtedly given him; instead, he had been jaunty and gay because he knew what he

28

had planted in the kitchen—and under the car; that had almost certainly been done during the night.

And that had not been a form of psychological terrorism; that would have blown him and Felicity to pieces.

The tramp's jaunty air would go with a laughing voice, too.

'Pat,' Felicity said, suddenly, 'what are we going to do if Joan doesn't come back soon?'

'We'll find her,' Dawlish said, gruffly. 'By now all the police in London and the Home Counties will be on the look-out for her. We'll find her before the day's out.'

They were empty words, and Felicity realized it as well as he did.

'How are you going to set about it?' she demanded.

The truth was, Dawlish didn't know. He needed time, and so did the police, yet there was so little to spare. First, Joan; then the telephone call from Exeter; then the explosion. He reminded himself that he could not be positive that the tramp had planted those explosives.

He said, 'I can't believe they'll injure Joan,' and again he realized how empty the words were.

'If Ivy or I had been in that doorway we would have been killed,' Felicity pointed out. 'It's no use blinking at facts, Pat; they mean to commit murder.' Then after a minute or two of silence, she added with a catch in her voice, 'I don't know what will happen to Ted if Joan's *been* murdered.'

This time, Dawlish did not answer.

It was half past twelve when they turned into Higham Mews, and the Beresfords' flat, in one corner of it, converted from an old coach house. Dawlish and Felicity had spent their war-time honeymoon at the flat; Dawlish, Beresford and Tim Jeremy had shared it whenever they had been on leave. It was small and homely, and full of memories. Ted had convalesced here after losing a leg in one of Dawlish's investigations. He and Joan had lived here for a long time now.

A police car stood outside the mews, and a policeman stood by the side of the car. Dawlish pulled up just behind it. Felicity was out before he was, and she hurried to the door while the policeman glanced at Dawlish, and recognized him.

'It's all right for you to go in, sir,' he said.

'Thanks. Is there any news of Mrs. Beresford?'

'Not what you'd call news, sir,' the policeman answered. 'I believe they've found her over-night case, though—floating in the Thames.'

## CHAPTER V

# NEWS

TED BERESFORD was a big man, quite as tall as, and rather broader than, Dawlish. Because his artificial leg limited his exercise, he was very heavy, too, having a much bigger paunch and being somewhat ungainly in movement. He was standing in the small living-room of the flat, the top of his head only a foot away from the ceiling, and when Felicity entered with Dawlish just behind her, he looked round.

Dawlish thought, 'He believes she's dead.'

This man, whom he had known for nearly forty years—for most of his life—looked as if despair was close upon him. His unruly dark hair, speckled with grey, showed where he had thrust his fingers through it time and time again. He was ugly in some ways, with rather big features and a heavy chin; the only time that he ever looked attractive was when he smiled. At the moment, it seemed likely to be a long time before he smiled again. There was something in the lifeless appearance of his brown eyes which alarmed Dawlish more than anything else. His face was very pale, too; even his lips looked grey. The lines at the sides of his mouth were deeply grooved, giving him vaguely the appearance of a bloodhound.

'Hallo, Fel,' he greeted, in a flat, deep tone.

'Ted, the worst can't have happened,' Felicity said in a strangled voice.

'Can't it, Fel?' Beresford still spoke tonelessly. His manner was almost aloof, obviously he was trying to conceal the depth of his feelings. 'This is Detective-Sergeant Plummer, who has just brought some of Joan's clothes from the Thames.' He stood aside. A thick sheet of rubber was lying over an armchair, the chair in which Joan usually sat and did her sewing. On this was a dress which had obviously been soaking in water and lightly wrung out, a pair of furlined slippers, a pair of brown leather house-shoes, some nylon stockings, a plastic toilet bag, a lightweight dressing-gown. There was something pathetic about the sight of their bedraggled shapelessness.

Felicity seemed to choke.

'All Joan's,' Beresford said. 'Bill Trivett looked in half an hour ago, and told me what they'd found. It was in the river near Chiswick Steps. Must have been there all night. Not exactly good, is it?'

'Not good,' Dawlish echoed hoarsely. 'What's Bill doing?'

'Having the river dragged. The Thames Division is out in force, G.P.O. engineers have had a look round, found that my telephone was cut—just beneath the window-ledge; there isn't much doubt that it was done to make sure I couldn't check on Joan, and she couldn't call me.'

'Anything else?' asked Dawlish.

'She caught the train at Oxford. Two people who knew her saw her. No one saw her get out at Paddington, the police are checking that now, Pat——' he broke off.

'Yes, Ted?'

Beresford looked away from Dawlish and Felicity. There was a savage note in his voice and a glitter in his eyes when he went on.

'Get Felicity out of here. Take her out of the country. Make sure there isn't a chance that she can be hurt. You'll be a bloody fool if you don't make her go.'

Dawlish said, 'I see what you mean'.

Beresford growled: 'You don't see what I mean. You think I'm wrong. You think the door will open and that Joan will walk in. Well, she won't. Don't ask me how I know, but she won't. I've worked with you on a hundred jobs, and there's always been plenty to worry about, but I've never felt like this. She's dead. I know it.' The burning glow was in his eyes again, and there were spots of colour at his cheeks. 'Don't take any risks with Felicity. You and I have a job to do, but she hasn't.'

After a pause, Felicity made herself say, 'You can't be sure yet, Ted.'

'No,' he said bitterly. 'I can't be sure. But if you were missing, and Joan were here, I'd put her on the first aircraft out of this country. I wouldn't tell anyone where she was going, and I wouldn't let her write to me or telephone me until I'd fixed Gorman and anyone else who is working with him. Joan wouldn't like it, but she would have to lump it. If you don't make Felicity go, Pat, it will be your own bloody fault.'

'Yes,' Dawlish said. 'I know.' He had to try something to ease the bleakness of Beresford's thoughts, had to start them running in different channels. 'We had some bother at the house, Ted. A johnny put nitro-glycerine or something like it in the kitchen doorway, and another dose under my car. No serious harm done, but we haven't a back entrance.

'Well, I've warned you,' Beresford said. He threw his chest

31

out and squared his shoulders, as if that was the only way he could breathe, and went on: 'Fel, if I sound like a heel, forget it. You've got to go away.'

She didn't answer.

'But I don't suppose you will, unless we knock you over the head and make you,' Beresford said. 'Let me tell you this: nothing you say or do will prevent Pat from going after Gorman.'

'I know, Ted,' Felicity said very matter-of-factly. 'I don't want to stop him, whether you're right about Joan or not. What are you going to do?'

'I wish to God I knew, just doing nothing burns me up. Gorman is still in Exeter—the Exeter Police actually spoke to him this morning. I've checked that with Trivett. We don't yet know anyone else who might be working with him. Until we get a lead from the Yard there isn't anything we can do, unless we go and help to drag the Thames.' He swung round savagely on the detective-sergeant, a tall, rather lean man who had been standing silent all the time. 'All set, Sergeant. I've identified the clothes, you can take 'em back.'

'Thank you, sir,' Sergeant Plummer said. 'I—er—I certainly wouldn't give up hope yet. It's quite usual for clothes to be thrown into a river or a lake in an effort to make it look as if——'

He faltered and broke off, because Beresford was staring at him fixedly, head a little to one side.

'Yes,' said Beresford. 'Thanks.' Suddenly, he pressed the heels of his thumbs against his forehead, and Dawlish saw how his face was twisted, how he was fighting against a breakdown; it seemed to Dawlish that Beresford was behaving as if he *knew* Joan was dead. Could he know? Would he behave like this simply because he 'felt in his bones' that the worst had happened? Ted was usually the most practical and prosaic of men, and was seldom impressed by presentiments.

The sergeant was gathering up the clothes.

'They've got the case at the Yard, testing it for finger-prints,' Beresford went on, 'but people who prepare a vendetta wouldn't be careless enough to leave prints around.' He watched the Yard man rolling up the clothes, then saw him to the door.

Dawlish and Felicity stood together in the living-room, Felicity pale and utterly at a loss, Dawlish feeling desperate in his longing to help.

They heard a car turn into the entrance of the mews.

32

Dawlish moved to the window, and saw Trivett's car. Everything that Beresford had said seemed to carry extra weight, for it was hard to believe that Trivett would come here unless he had news, and had it been good, he would surely have telephoned.

'Pat, if Joan is——' Felicity began.

'Let's work that one out when we know for certain,' Dawlish interrupted huskily. He went towards the narrow passage, saw Beresford standing at the heard of the steps and staring towards the Yard man, and felt sure that Beresford believed this was confirmation of all that he feared. Trivett's car, a black Rover, stopped. Beresford started to go down the steps, clumsily, and Dawlish followed him, so that they saw Trivett get out of the car.

Dawlish felt a stab of dismay at Trivett's expression. The Yard man came walking across the cobbles, looking straight at Beresford. Dawlish heard Felicity move, just behind him, and felt her touch his arm. Trivett reached the foot of the steps, as Beresford said harshly:

'Well?'

'Ted,' said Trivett, as if it were very difficult to get words out, 'I'm afraid it couldn't be worse.'

Felicity's finger dug into Dawlish's arm.

It seemed to Dawlish that Beresford swayed a little. Dawlish hurried down the steps to be by his side. He saw Beresford's hands bunch into great fists. He heard his friend breathing heavily through his nostrils.

'Drowned?' he asked, flatly.

'No,' answered Trivett. He was as close a friend of Beresford as he was of Dawlish; he had known both men for twenty years, as he had known Joan; and he and his wife had often been here. 'No,' he repeated. 'Strangled, Ted, there's no doubt at all that it happened very quickly.'

Beresford didn't answer. Dawlish felt wholly, utterly despairing, for now all hope had been torn away, and Beresford was in the abyss of grief.

Trivett went on, hesitating over each word: 'She was found in the river, south of Chiswick Steps. There was no sign of injury except the marks of fingers at her throat.'

Beresford seemed to whisper, '*Fingers?*'

'It was manual strangulation.'

'God!' breathed Beresford. He seemed to choke. He raised his great hands, the fingers unclenching, but curved still like talons. He held them a little way in front of him, as if he would encircle someone's neck. 'God!' he breathed again. 'I'll kill the swine with my own hands.'

Dawlish felt sweat stinging his forehead, felt horror crawl in the pit of his stomach.

'Bill,' he managed to ask, 'have you found out anything else?'

Trivett nodded.

'What?' Dawlish demanded. He saw Beresford's eyes burning, saw that his crooked fingers seemed to be tightening, as if in his imagination he could feel the throat of the killer he would set out to kill.

'There was a big old Austin hackney carriage,' Trivett answered. 'It was seen round the corner from here about half past six last night, parked for ten minutes or so. A similar car was seen close to Chiswick Steps about seven o'clock last night. She—she floated only fifty yards from the spot where she was thrown in. There's not much current just there, everything fetches up near the steps. We've got the tyre-marks of the car as well as a description, and we know that there were two men.' When neither Dawlish nor Beresford spoke, Trivett went on: 'A couple were walking along the river bank at the time, and saw the car. The woman is married, and didn't want anything said, that's why she was so late coming forward. So we've made a start.'

Dawlish said, 'We want to see those tyre tracks.'

'No reason why not,' responded Trivett. His gaze settled on Beresford for several moments, and it was as if he knew that anything which might ease Beresford's tension, anything which would give him something to do, would be his one way of helping, now. 'I've arranged with the Chiswick people to let you and Ted have any facilities you want. We'll do everything we possibly can.'

Then Beresford spoke.

He did so slowly, turning round towards Felicity, pushing Dawlish a little to one side. His eyes were burning and the set of his lips made him look anguished beyond all words.

'So you'll do everything you can,' he said. 'All right. Start at once. This minute. Take Felicity away. Lock her up, send her out of the country, do anything you like, but take her away. You can't trust Pat to; you can't trust her not to want to stay. If you don't, if you let anything happen to her, it will mean that Joan died for nothing at all. At least she can still save Felicity,'

He broke off.

34

Then he burst out: '*Oh, God, Joan! Oh, God!*' and he covered his face with his hands.

CHAPTER VI

## NEED

'HE MUST have something to do,' Felicity said. 'That's the one thing he needs. You must do something, Pat.'

'Yes,' Dawlish said, and looked at her sideways. 'I've other problems, too.'

'What problems?'

'You.'

Felicity didn't answer.

'Gorman's had one go at you, and he might have another at any moment,' Dawlish went on. 'Ted's quite right, and you can't help him simply by being around.'

Felicity just looked at him.

Ted Beresford and Trivett were in the bedroom, talking. Soon they would go to the morgue for formal identification, and that was going to be the most difficult time of all. Dawlish found it hard to think beyond that; his mind seemed clogged by the shock and the suddenness of it all. One thing was becoming vividly clear, though.

He said, 'You know you've got to go away, don't you?'

Felicity answered, very slowly.

'Yes, I suppose so.' Heavily: 'I suppose I'll have to, if only for Ted's sake. But I can't leave the country. I've got to be close at hand, in case . . .'

She didn't finish.

'We'll find somewhere handy,' Dawlish said gruffly. 'Where we're not known, where they can't find you. Trivett will fix it for us. There—there isn't any point in coming with Ted and me on the next trip.'

'No,' agreed Felicity. 'Yet I'd like—I'd like to see her, Pat.'

He nearly said, 'Later,' and thought, 'Oh God, in her coffin'; and then realized that if Felicity were to go to safety she must go at once: ahead lay strange, unfamiliar things: the funeral, the mourning, the fight against—who? *Was* it Gorman? For the first time Dawlish saw and considered another possibility: that someone else who knew that Gorman was being released from prison early had timed the attacks

35

to coincide with the obvious suspect. Was that feasible? Who would know, except the prison authorities? Why fool himself? Dawlish made himself ask: convicts on the Moor got to know everything on the grape-vine, and had plenty of ways of sending information out; hundreds of people might have chosen this moment, there was still no certainty that it was Gorman.

Trivett and Ted came out, Ted looking even more untidy, his hair rumpled, his eyes starkly bright. His face still had an unhealthy pallor, and the lines at his lips and chin seemed more deeply etched.

'Bill,' Felicity greeted them, 'can you find somewhere for me to stay for a few days?'

Beresford's eyes actually lit up.

'Yes, of course,' said Trivett. 'There won't be any difficulty about that.'

'It mustn't be too far away, I must be able to telephone Pat daily.'

'Yes,' said Trivett, and assured her again: 'There'll be no difficulty.'

'Where will it be?' asked Dawlish.

Trivett said, 'I'm not sure yet, Pat.' But obviously he had been thinking about this, for he went on quickly: 'I think the best thing will be for Felicity to come to the Yard with me, and we'll fix her up with a policewoman's uniform or something as hideous, so that she can't be recognized when she leaves.' He gave a quick, bleak smile. 'How does that sound?'

It sounded as if Trivett felt quite sure that there would be an attack on Felicity, so he feared the worst. And Felicity understood exactly how deep the implications went, and how acute the danger was for Dawlish. There was a moment of great tension. Beresford broke it, giving an unnatural kind of grin, putting a hand on Felicity's shoulder and squeezing hard enough to hurt.

'That's my girl,' he said. 'That's a load off my mind. And what are you looking so down-in-the-mouth for? It isn't the first time you've been separated from your dear hubby. Like to remember some of the other times? On twenty-seven occasions, parachuted behind the enemy lines in France, Italy and Germany. Each time the chances were far worse than fifty-fifty, and he hardly got a scratch. As many times again under threat from men quite as bad as Gorman. Pat had his nine lives a decade ago, he's on the way to his ninety-ninth. He's going to die with his boots off, lying in bed with you nursing him up to the last gasp, so you needn't start fretting about that now.' There was a rough edge to Beresford's voice, and the pressure of his fingers became more painful, but Felicity did not flinch. 'I'm going along to see Joan. Coming, Pat?'

'We're both coming,' Felicity said.

Beresford looked down at her from his six feet two; a smile curved his lips again, and there was a softening in his eyes.

'Yes,' he said. 'Of course. Thanks, Fel.'

* * * * *

The underground room was cool. Except for bright lights which shone above the cold stone slabs, where were gloom and shadows. The morgue keeper walked with a limp and hobbled towards one of two slabs which were occupied. Felicity was between the two men. Beresford reached his wife's body first, and very slowly pulled the corner of the sheet which covered her face.

There lay Joan, as serene as if she were asleep.

Her face was untouched, there was not even a scratch; and about her neck there were loosely coiled bandages, obviously there to hide the bruises.

After a long, long pause, Beresford said in a strangely calm voice:

'All right, sweet. I'll get him. I'll do to him what he did to you. That's a promise.'

None of the others spoke, but Dawlish saw Trivett looking at him intently, and felt sure that he knew what Trivett was thinking. Beresford had to be allowed to work, day and night, in the search for the murderer, but he must be saved from killing the killer. The law said so.

Beresford drew back the sheet to hide Joan's face.

'All right,' he went on, jerkily. 'Queer situation, isn't it? How long have we been married? Fifteen years. That's a hell of a long time.' He led the way towards the door, still talking. 'The man who killed her has a lot to answer for; at least another twenty-five years or more of happiness. How do you make a man suffer for robbing you of twenty-five years? How do you put him in hell?'

* * * * *

They turned into Scotland Yard, Dawlish in the front with Trivett, Beresford and Felicity behind. Dawlish found himself looking at everyone nearby, especially those who loitered, and at the back of his mind there was the image of the face of the tramp. He saw no one remotely like the man. They got out, watched by a dozen detectives in the Yard as well as half a dozen uniformed men, and everyone recognized Dawlish and Beresford. Every eye was sympathetic, but no one spoke to them. They went up in the lift to Trivett's office, which overlooked the Thames and the Embankment. The sun shimmered off the river, and the world looked bright and gay. Trivett went to his desk and picked up several reports, read them, and glanced up at the men.

'An old hackney carriage licence plate's been found near the spot where the suitcase was, half-buried in the mud. That looks as if it was tied on to the Austin to fool anyone who saw it—we're not necessarily looking for a hackney. But they can't alter the tyre-prints.

'They can change the tyres,' Beresford interpolated, 'and put them on the scrap-heap. What are the chances of finding the car?'

'Poor,' Trivett answered bluntly. 'There's something else . . . Haslemere reports that your maid isn't badly hurt, Pat, and has been sent to her home in Alum. There are two men on duty at the house and will be until you go back—a day-and-night watch. The packet you took away from the wheel of your car was filled with nitro-glycerine, and the packet itself is made of highly inflammable plastic-stuff impregnated with cellulose. You and anyone in the car would have been blown sky-high.'

He did not change his tone as he said that, and the quietness of the statement added to the horror of it. Felicity moved to the window and looked out on to the smiling river, and Dawlish glanced at her and wished that there was something more he could do.

'Good job you kept your wits about you,' Beresford said. 'Nice work, Pat.'

'Anything about that tramp?' inquired Dawlish.

'No, and that's rather a peculiar thing,' Trivett answered. He held out a typewritten memo, and Dawlish took it, then he and Beresford read it together. All the inhabitants of Alum Village and everyone in outlying cottages and the nearest farm had been questioned, but none of them had seen a tramp of any kind that morning. There were two reports that a small car had pulled up not far from Four Ways, and that a man had walked from the car towards the house, but only the top of the man's head had been seen.

'Grey-haired,' Dawlish said, softly. 'That's the joke. He came in a car, and he came just to see us. Will you ask Haslemere to try to pick up a description of the car, Bill?'

'We won't miss a trick,' Trivett assured him. 'And here's another thing.' He picked up a small plastic envelope, and inside it was a twisted piece of black insulation tape. He held it up to the light as Felicity turned away from the river, and said: 'This is the telephone cable at your place, Ted, the piece which was damaged. There's one fingerprint on a piece of insulation tape used to stick the cut cable to the wall so that no one was likely to notice it was broken. Sooner or later we'll find that useful.'

'Had it photographed?' demanded Dawlish.

'Yes, of course.'

'Let Ted and me have a print, will you?'

'Yes.'

'Something to search for,' Beresford remarked. 'That's the spirit—keep me occupied.' He gave the fierce grin again. 'Come on, Bill, let's leave the love-birds together to say their *au revoir*.' He moved towards the door:

'Thanks,' said Dawlish. 'Where are you going to take her, Bill?'

'I still don't know,' answered Trivett, rather too casually.

Dawlish started to say: 'Now, listen——' and then closed his lips, to trap the words. Trivett did not intend that he should know where Felicity was going to hide, and nothing could make the Yard's opinion of the gravity of the situation more vivid. He was probably right, too, for there could come a time when the knowledge would be dangerous. That was almost worth a laugh! Beresford raised a hand to his lips, blew Felicity a kiss and said:

'Thanks again, Fel.'

'It won't be long,' Felicity said.

'With the great Patrick Dawlish and his trusty henchman, hardly any time at all,' declared Beresford. He turned his back on her, and went out, with Trivett on his heels. Felicity stood with her back to the window and the sunshine, so that it was difficult to see her expression.

'You know, Ted's right,' Dawlish said. 'This isn't exactly our baptism.'

'I think it's the first time that you and Bill Trivett have felt that I must be hidden away,' said Felicity, quietly. She came towards him. 'Pat, you won't take a single avoidable chance, will you?'

39

'No.'

'And you won't let Ted——'

'I won't let Ted kill anyone in cold blood, if I can help it.'

'He scares me,' said Felicity, very slowly. 'I've never seen him or anyone else look like it.'

'I know,' Dawlish said, as slowly. 'It's partly shock. After he's had a bit of action, he'll feel better. Fel, every minute we spend here now will add a minute on to the other end. Take Bill's advice. I'll keep him posted as to where I am, so you'll always know where to find me. If I'm out of range for a few hours, don't start thinking the worst.' He took her in his arms. 'It'll work out, you know; it always has.'

'I know,' Felicity said.

\* \* \* \* \*

She felt the great power of Pat's arms and the strength in his body as he held her close. Then he kissed her, long and fiercely, and set her aside. He smiled, making her feel for one supreme moment that she was the only person in the world. He turned and went out, massive, broad and brisk-moving, and slanting sunlight shone on his flaxen hair. He didn't look round from the door. He closed it, with a snap, and there was a kind of finality about that. She gave a little, uncontrollable shiver. She knew him so well, and knew that now that the door was closed on her, he would put her out of his mind while he worked to find the man who had killed Joan.

It was as if he had shut her out of his life.

She hated the thought, but knew that it was true.

Then the door opened and Trivett came in, alone.

## CHAPTER VII

### FIRST CALL

'WELL,' said Beresford. 'Where, and what?' He pushed his fingers through his thick, unruly hair, and went on: 'I've got to see Joan's mother. That's the first job. I needn't stay long, her sister will stand in for me there. There are the formalities, too.' He still spoke in that cold, flat voice. 'We'll work from the flat, of course.'

'Yes,' Dawlish said.

'You haven't yet told me where or what,' went on Beresford. 'You are still the brains of this outfit.' He stood on the corner of Parliament Square, with the traffic surging about them, while Dawlish watched all the passers-by, especially a small man who had been coming out of a shop on the corner when they had walked from Scotland Yard into Parliament Street. The little man was not taking any particular notice of them, but Dawlish made sure that he would recognize him again; if he reappeared, he would be worth questioning. 'We can't leave everything to the Yard,' Beresford went on. 'Trivett promised that he would let us have the names and addresses of anyone else who might want to cut your throat and mine, but it may be a day before we get them.' When Dawlish still didn't answer, Beresford went on in a rougher voice: 'Pat, get one thing clear. I'm not going to be side-tracked. I know what all of you think—that I mustn't be let loose on the killer. Don't try to stop me.'

'I won't try to stop you,' Dawlish promised. 'You could be forgetting something, Ted. I want to get him both for what he has done and what he might do. The first thing is to try to make sure that it's Gorman.'

'I'm sure.'

'Ted, we can't work on hunches or on guesswork,' Dawlish reasoned. 'All we know is that there was a man on the telephone with a laugh in his voice, and two men with an old Austin. There's one thing Trivett told us which is worth thinking about, though, and which might help us a lot.'

'What?'

'The only person who visited Gorman in prison was his sister-in-law.'

'Oh,' Beresford said. 'Yes. I didn't think of that.'

'It's a long way from London to Dartmoor,' Dawlish pointed out, almost inanely. 'The sister-in-law went down there three or four times most years. I doubt if that was out of a sense of duty. It ought to be worth finding out why, so— call Number One is on Eileen Parish.'

'How do you know her name?'

'I had time to look through the dossier I'd made up on Gorman,' Dawlish said. 'It's in the Allard, now, in the suitcase. He saw a taxi approach, with its *For Hire* sign alight. 'Taxi, or legs?'

'Legs.'

'Right,' said Dawlish, with satisfaction.

They set out, striding. Beresford could make a good speed on level ground, in spite of his limp, and they crossed Parliament Square and then walked through St. James's Park,

41

without saying a word. There were half a dozen young children and a few adults near the pond, but more ducks than people. The sun glistened on the neck feathers of a drake which preened itself. Now and again Dawlish glanced round, but saw no sign of the little man; that did not necessarily mean that the man had not been interested in them. He kept thinking about the tramp and those shiny brown shoes; every man with brown shoes drew his eye.

They reached the Mall, and Beresford said:

'Let's get a cab now.'

'Good idea,' Dawlish agreed.

It was nearly three o'clock when they reached the mews. The Allard was standing where Dawlish had left it, and a uniformed policeman reported, 'No one's been near it, sir.'

'Thanks,' said Dawlish, and opened the boot.

He had not a moment's warning of what was to come. Instantly, there was a vivid flash and a sharp crack of sound, and only the top of the boot saved his face from the fierce flame. As he staggered back, terror struck savagely at him. He heard Beresford shouting questions and the policeman calling out, and felt himself dragged to one side.

The flash had dazzled, not blinded him, and soon he saw the Yard man playing an extinguisher on to the fire, which was nearly out. The stench of the foam was in Dawlish's nostrils. He saw Beresford lifting the suitcase out, using thick gloves, and went to him.

The case was damaged, but the contents were not. Once they were sure of that, the men went into the flat. Beresford was clenching his teeth, as if to keep back pain, while the menace of an attack out of the blue was heavy upon them both.

'We need a snack,' Beresford made himself say. 'I can rustle up some sandwiches, with ham or cheese. The larder's low, I was leaving Joan to fix that this morning. You take your things out of the bag, and get Felicity's clobber over to the Yard.' He limped out of the room, for his disability always showed up more whenever he was gloomy or tired.

Dawlish kept wondering how the explosive had been put in the car; it had not been a lethal one, like the sachet, probably because the nitro-glycerine was so dangerous to handle. He had stopped at several traffic lights on the way, three of them just before getting to the mews, and as he had not expected to park, had not locked the boot. There had been time for someone to open it and put in the booby trap, which

42

had been set off when the lid opened. It need have taken only a few seconds, while they were stationary—and at most traffic lights Dawlish had turned to look at Felicity.

He was looking towards the door when the telephone bell rang. He moved towards the window, where the instrument stood on a low table, called, 'I'll get it, Ted,' and lifted the receiver. 'This is Mr. Edward Beresford's home,' he announced.

A man chuckled.

Dawlish felt his nerves go tense.

'And that is Mr. Patrick Dawlish speaking,' the man said brightly. 'You've had quite an active morning, haven't you? But I think I can promise you that you will have a lot more activity in the future. Tell me—why did you leave your wife at Scotland Yard? Don't say that she is going to be charged with some heinous crime.' The speaker paused before going on in the same chuckling way: 'What's wrong, Mr. Dawlish? Are you too full for words?'

'Not exactly,' Dawlish said. 'You've moved pretty fast from Exeter, haven't you?'

'You have to move fast in my profession,' the man replied. 'Executioners are such a misunderstood breed of men! Evasion won't help, you know—we'll find your wife!'

He rang off.

Dawlish put the receiver down slowly, and turned to see Ted with a hunk of white bread in one hand and a saw-edged knife in the other.

'Who?' Ted demanded.

'The man who called me from Exeter,' Dawlish answered, and thought bleakly: 'The man who laughs at murder.' He went on with pretended assurance: 'He's simply trying to get us on the hop, Ted, as with that booby-trap. He'll keep at it all the time.'

Beresford seemed to explode.

'I'd give my life to catch him!'

'We'll catch him,' said Dawlish, and tried not to be alarmed because the caller knew that Felicity had stayed behind at the Yard. 'It's got to be soon,' he added grimly. 'If it's not they'll get us on the run.'

Dawlish picked up the London telephone book with the L to R letters in it, and went into the kitchen. Ted finished making sandwiches, using the knife with savage slashes, as Dawlish thumbed through the pages, then ran his forefinger down a column. He looked up, and said: 'Parish, Eileen S.,

17 Mountjoy Street, Chelsea. That's her ladyship, I remember the address. Ted, I——'

The telephone rang again, bringing sudden, frightening tension; but this time it was Beresford's sister.

Beresford could not put off the Oxford trip any longer, much though he hated the need for Dawlish to visit Gorman's sister-in-law by himself. But Dawlish felt an easing of tension when Beresford started off at the wheel of his ancient Bentley, a bright green one which looked as if it had been made for race-tracks of a decade ago, and sounded like an underdeveloped jet. He saw Ted swing out of the mews, and a little car on the other side of the road had to move sharply out of the way. Ted was vicious, bitter, hating, desperate—dangerous.

Those emotions and his grief would destroy his judgement.

Dawlish thought, 'Somehow I've got to hold on to mine.'

He called Trivett, and checked that there was no fresh news. He said nothing about going to Eileen Parish, sure that Trivett would make some formal protest about his working on his own. Even without the sense of personal involvement, he would have worked without the police. From his first venture into investigating crimes, the feeling that everything he did was being watched by the police had a kind of claustrophobic effect on him; without it he had a sense of freedom and greater scope. In many ways team-work had its uses, but it could also hold one back.

Felicity was safe; Ted had to see Joan's mother; he, Dawlish, could make this first move free from anxiety about them.

He drove out of the mews in the Allard, brooding over Joan, thinking with increasing vexation about the brief-case, wondering whether he had been followed from Four Ways or whether the car had been picked up somewhere on the outskirts of London. The one certain and even frightening aspect was the thoroughness with which Gorman was carrying out the campaign.

*If* it were Gorman.

Eileen Parish was certainly Gorman's sister-in-law.

As he neared King's Road, Chelsea, knowing that Mountjoy Street lay between here and the river, Dawlish found himself wondering about the woman. He had never seen her and there had never been any need to find out what she looked like. If she were in, he would soon know. He pulled up outside a house in a long, curving terrace, out of sight of but not far from the river. A few cars were parked on either side. The pointed roofs of the houses made a dark serration like dragon's teeth against the vivid blue of the sky, for as the sun began to sink lower in the horizon it drained less colour away. He looked up and down. No one appeared to have taken any notice of him, no one appeared to have followed. It was possible that Trivett had arranged for radio police cars to report on his movements, but he could worry about that later.

He approached the front door of Number 17. There was no name plate outside, and nothing to suggest that this house was broken up into flats or was a boarding house like many of them here. There was only one bell. He pressed it, but did not hear it ring. He stood back, looking upwards and telling himself that this could easily be a wasted journey; after all, the sister-in-law might have acted out of a sense of duty. This looked like a family house, and Eileen Parish would probably turn out to be a matronly soul with a brood of children; he was not even sure whether the name Parish was hers by marriage or birth.

There was no answer.

Dawlish stood back, looked up at the first floor, and noticed that two windows were slightly open at the top. He glanced round, and saw no one at the windows of the houses opposite. He rang the bell again, but already his thoughts were beginning to tick over very fast, and he knew exactly what he must do. It was a good, not a bad, thing that the house was empty.

And his mind was working again!

He studied the Yale lock of the door. There were two methods of forcing such locks, but only one way would leave this one undamaged; for that, he needed tools. He could force the lock with the steel blade of his knife, one made of a special tensile steel used in the far-off days when his life had sometimes depended on being able to pick a lock or slit a throat without being burdened with an awkward weapon.

He slid the point of the blade between the door and the frame, and pushed it slowly so that the flexible blade crept round the edge of the door. Quite suddenly he heard a click, and the door sagged open. He drew back, glanced about him, and now noticed an elderly woman standing at the window of a house opposite. Two children were playing along the street, and a post-office van sped round a corner. Dawlish rang the door-bell again, and a moment later doffed his hat at the closed door, which he pushed open a few inches with his hat. He paused, lowered his hat to his side, and stepped into the hall. He took his knife from the lock, then closed the door quickly. He could not be sure that the woman on the other side of the street had been fooled, so he stepped swiftly into the front room of this house. The only sound was the squeak of the door and the creak of his footsteps. There were long, lace curtains, and he could not be seen from outside. He saw the woman still standing at the window; nothing suggested that she had seen any cause for alarm.

He turned round.

This was the drawing-room of a house larger than it had seemed from the outside, well furnished in a rather old-fashioned way, with heavy, red mahogany furniture, a large mirror over the ornate fireplace, very comfortable-looking saddle-back chairs, even a saddle-back sofa. There were some oil portraits on the walls, none of which he recognized. On the small baby grand piano were several photographs, and he looked at each in turn.

One was of Maurice Gorman.

His wife was dead; his son was dead; why was he himself remembered in this house fondly enough to have that photograph on the piano? Certainly there was no sense of shame.

He turned to the door and, doing so, heard a noise upstairs, a faint thump of sound. He stood rigidly still, staring up at the ceiling, and the sound was repeated.

## CHAPTER VIII

### SISTER-IN-LAW

DAWLISH stepped into the passage which led to the stairs and to the domestic quarters beyond. There were two doors in the drawing-room, and no danger that anyone would come out of that room. He went with his long, swift strides towards the domestic quarters, thrust open the door of a small room—probably a maid's sitting-room in the old days—and then the kitchen itself. It was large, oblong and very modern in scarlet and black. Beyond it was a scullery where he saw a large washing-machine and a spin-drier.

The back door was locked, but not bolted. He shot the bolt at the top, then went back into the passage and locked every door on the ground floor, leaving the keys on the outside. He heard another faint thud. He reached the front door pushed it close, shot the bolts and put a chain into position;

from the outside no one could get in, and no one could tell the lock had been tampered with.

He started up a long, narrow flight of carpeted stairs which had a shiny banister rail. At the first landing this curved round so that there was a well which ran straight down from the third, top floor to the ground floor. He heard the noise again. He reached the first floor and stood, touching the highly polished banister, until he identified the direction of the sound. It was from the room behind him, the one over the front end of the drawing-room.

There were three other doors on this landing, and he stepped to each, glanced inside a bathroom, a bedroom and what looked like a small office or study. He closed and locked these doors, stepped swiftly along to the front room, and could hear the thudding much more clearly. The door was ajar. He stood to one side, stretched out his right leg so that his toe was against the bottom of the door, and kicked. The door swung open, but nothing else happened. It banged against the wall and swung back slowly, stopping when it was half-open.

He saw a large dressing-table in the big bay window, a tall wardrobe against the wall immediately ahead of him—and in the mirror the reflection of a woman lying on a double bed.

She was bound to the sides of the old-fashioned bed by the wrists and by the ankles, so that she lay spreadeagled; and she was stark naked.

She was staring at the door, and Dawlish realized that she had made that bumping sound by banging her head against the shiny head-board; she could not make any other sound, for a patch of adhesive plaster had been stuck over her lips. It made her look grotesque, although her hair was dark and curly, and her figure was that of a young woman, beautifully formed.

He stepped inside and she let her head fall back on the pillows. That way she could only just see Dawlish, by half-closing her eyes and looking at him through her lashes. He stood with a hand at the door, and then said in a casual voice:

'I'll be back in a jiffy.'

He turned towards the landing, telling himself that this could not be a coincidence, it had the hallmarks of a frame-up. It was useless to tell himself that no one could have guessed that this was where he would first come; it had happened, and he would have to find the explanation of it later. Now he had to make sure that no one could come in here and accuse him of assaulting the woman. It might be wise to telephone the police at once, but he had to take some risk, and he wanted to question the woman before the police came.

He ran up the next flight of stairs to another landing; there were the same number of doors as below. He glanced into three bedrooms and a bathroom, got the impression that none of these rooms was used very often, closed and locked the big doors, then looked up at a loft hatch. The cover of this was closed, but there was a bolt which had not been shot home. He could just reach it. He jumped up several times, making sure the bolt was tightly fast, and was now certain that every possible entry to the house was barred, so he went down the stairs again.

He did not find it difficult to picture the woman as she lay there. He called out:

'I'm on my way,' and stepped inside. As he passed the wardrobe he opened it, took out the first coat which came to hand, a rich dark-brown fur, warm to touch, and he draped this carelessly over the woman. He stood and smiled wryly down at her. 'Quite a situation,' he observed. 'Do you have any medical spirit in the house?' As he spoke he bent down and studied the way her wrists were tied. A thick string, not a cord, had been wound round the wrist and then tied round the iron frame of the bedstead; she had a little freedom of movement, but if the red marks at the wrist were anything to go by she had tried hard to move. There was gooseflesh on her arms.

Dawlish glanced up, and she nodded an answer to his question.

'Good,' he said. 'Now I'll cut you loose. There's room for a knife, it won't hurt.' He took out his knife and the blade glinted; it was nearly four o'clock, and the slanting rays of the sun were brilliant and made the scene vivid. He placed the blade of the knife flat against the woman's wrist, and the edge against the string, then sawed until the strands parted. He did the same at the other side, then with her ankles. She did not immediately move her arms or legs; she wouldn't be able to if they were stiff, and they would be if she had been like that for any length of time. But she shivered violently.

How long had she been like that? How confident could anyone have been that he would come here?

'Shouldn't try to move too much,' he advised. 'I'll try a little massage when I've got that spirit. Is it in the bathroom?'

She nodded.

She had clear eyes, eyes the colour and the beauty of a chestnut just out of its spiky husk. He thought, vaguely, that she was probably a few years younger than Felicity or Joan. He knew that his expression changed, and bleakness took possession of him.

'Is it in the bathroom on this floor?'

She nodded again.

'I won't be long,' he promised, and went to the fireplace, switched on an electric fire, and went out. He turned the key in the bathroom door, but did not go inside immediately. Although he believed that he had taken all possible precautions he felt a pressing sense of danger. But the bathroom was empty. There were two cabinets, one flush with a wall opposite the old-fashioned bath, the other in a corner, and on this was a small red cross. He opened the door, saw the two shelves crowded with bottles, tins and bandages, everything needed for first aid. A small glass bottle marked *Surgical Spirit* was half full. He took an opened roll of cotton wool, went back to the bedroom, and found that the woman had drawn one arm and one leg underneath the fur coat. He made himself grin at her.

'Better? You will be, soon.' He hitched up a chair and sat down, the heat of the fire on him. 'The idea is to soak this plaster with the spirit and leave it for a few minutes. It's a solvent for the gooey stuff which makes the plaster stick.' He poured spirit on to a piece of cotton-wool and then began to dab it; the sharp, almost suffocating smell made the woman gasp, and she began to heave for breath.

He saw not her face but Joan's, for Joan must have heaved and fought far more desperately than this. His mouth set very tightly. The woman turned her head this way and that, but it was several seconds before she began to breathe normally. When he could bring himself to look at her again there were tears in her eyes. He put on a little more of the spirit, and this time the effect was less painful. He drew back, seeing that her face was becoming pink from the warmth of the fur and the fire.

'I'll try it now,' he said, and picked at one corner of the plaster and began to pull. Only twice did it stick; each time he pulled a little harder, and it came away without trouble. He was careful not to touch too much of the outside of the plaster, but put it down carefully on the dressing-table, then turned round to look at the woman. Three or four tiny specks of blood were showing where the skin had broken, and the rest of the place where the patch had been was red and angry looking.

'Do you know who did this?' he asked.

She shook her head, and began to move her lips, as if trying to get some blood into them; when the blood began to circulate, she would really be in pain. Dawlish took her right wrist and began to rub it vigorously, round and round; he let it fall, and then massaged the other wrist. Her eyes began to twitch, as if with pain; she kept wincing, and her lips writhed. He could understand exactly what was happening, this wasn't an act. After a few minutes she screwed up her eyes tightly, and didn't open them again for a long time; she kept her lips set tightly too, as if that was the only way in which she could prevent herself from crying out. He moved towards the end of the bed and began to massage her ankles. She had quite beautiful legs, and the cord there had been tied less tightly.

'I'm going to make you some tea,' he announced suddenly. 'See if you can wriggle under the bedclothes. I'll pull some out from under you.'

She didn't respond as he tugged until she had a chance to get beneath the sheet.

He made a quick check of all the doors, to be sure they were closed and locked, then hurried down to the kitchen. He tried not to think, just let thoughts and possibilities drift through his mind, but all the time one question was most urgent: *Why had this been done to her?*

Would Gorman have attacked his own sister-in-law like it? Would he have allowed others to? Remember she was the only person who had visited him in Dartmoor.

Dawlish filled an electric kettle, switched on and looked out of the kitchen window. A wide service road fed the back of this street and the one which ran parallel, and at the end of each garden was a shed or a garage; there was a single door leading to the garage at the end of this one. He found the tea and cups, saucers, milk and sugar, then went into the garden. The garage door was unlocked. He opened it, and stared at an old car, its nose and radiator facing him.

It was a big black Austin, about fifteen years old.

'Well, well,' he said softly. He hesitated for a moment, then squeezed between the side of the car and the wooden wall of the garage, and checked that the double doors leading to the service road were locked and bolted. He found an electric-light switch, and pressed it down. Along one wall was a narrow bench, a few tools and the kind of oddments which a motorist would keep by him. Everything was spick and span. He scanned a shelf, and saw a small roll of half-inch insulation tape on it, black like the tape which had been used to stick Beresford's telephone cable to the wall.

He wrapped this up in his handkerchief, then knelt down and looked at the tyres. They were Dunlops, and might well be those which had made the tyre-prints near Chiswick steps. He glanced back to the kitchen and saw that the kettle was boiling furiously; the window was steaming up. 'Blast it!' he muttered, and ran back, switched the kettle off, and then returned to the car; nothing must delay him from looking inside.

The light was good.

He saw several long hairs, dark and greying and believed that they were Joan's. With great care he picked up six or seven, took out his wallet, selected an envelope containing a letter which he had received a few days ago, and folded the hairs inside it. That done, he returned to the house. He called up from the kitchen door:

'*Won't be a jiff*,' but there was no answer. He made the tea, took it to the stairs, then hurried to the big room and went straight to a beautiful marquetry cabinet. He opened this and found whisky and brandy. He stuffed a bottle of each into his pockets, so that they bulged awkwardly, took one glass and put this on the tea-tray and went upstairs.

The woman had managed to wriggle so that some of the bedclothes were over her, and the coat was on top of her too; only her bare right shoulder showed. She looked flushed and there was rather more blood at her lips, in tiny little globules. The worst of the pain must have gone, and she turned her head more easily to look at him as he set the tray down on a bedside table.

'Better?' he asked, formally.

For the first time he heard her speak; her husky voice seemed to come only with a great effort.

'Yes,' she said. 'Thank you—thank you very much.' She paused, and as Dawlish began to pour out tea she went on: 'Aren't you—aren't you Patrick Dawlish?'

'Yes.'

'What——' she began.

He turned round, with a cup of tea in his hand. She wriggled up, manoeuvring a sheet so that it covered her up to

51

the neck, and took the cup. It rattled a little in the saucer. He watched as she put both cup and saucer on the table, and then lifted the cup. She kept looking at what she was doing, and then at him as if she was bursting to ask questions.

Dawlish said: 'Your brother-in-law killed Joan Beresford last night. Where is he?'

## CHAPTER IX

## SHOCK?

THE woman on the bed nearly dropped the cup. A little tea spilled over the side and spread over the white sheet. Her eyes rounded as if with shock, and she drew in a gasping breath. It was impossible to be sure whether her reaction was genuine or not, but certainly it looked as if she were badly shocked.

'It—it's impossible,' she asserted. 'He——' She broke off, hesitated, then put the cup down on the saucer. She hitched herself up higher, and did not worry because the sheet slipped down. 'It's impossible,' she repeated in a stronger voice. 'He was in—in prison last night.'

'That's why I've come to see you,' Dawlish said. 'Who did you hire to do it for him?'

If she had poured out denials he would have wondered whether she was protesting too much, but she simply stared, the effect of the shock still showing in her eyes. They were slightly bloodshot, and she was much more flushed than before.

'Well, who did it for Gorman?' Dawlish demanded.

'I—I know absolutely nothing about it. You mean—you mean your friend *Beresford's* wife?'

'You remember her well,' Dawlish said, stonily.

'I—I remember the whole thing vividly,' answered Gorman's sister-in-law. 'It was a hideous experience, and——' She broke off. 'Murdered,' she whispered, as if the real significance of what Dawlish had said had only just struck home. 'Oh, *no*.'

'In your car,' Dawlish said, harshly.

'No!' She sat up more, and was quite oblivious. 'No, that's impossible.'

'It happened.'

'I can't believe——' She broke off and closed her eyes and then belatedly drew up the sheet. After a long pause she went on: 'Mr. Dawlish, I'm terribly sorry. I can understand how you feel, but I can assure you that I had nothing at all to do with it, and I am quite sure that Maurice hadn't.'

'If you've such a good memory, you remember what he said he would do,' said Dawlish, still in a stony voice. 'He's started.'

'I simply don't believe it.'

'Do you know what evidence is?' demanded Dawlish. 'Evidence is the thing which gets people hanged. There's positive evidence that Joan Beresford was in your car last night, and strong circumstantial evidence that she was killed in it. Where were you?'

'I—I was—I was out.'

'Where?'

'I was at a—a cinema. I'd been to the West End first.'

Dawlish said, roughly, 'Even you don't expect me to believe that one.'

She didn't answer.

He said, 'You'd better drink that tea while it's hot.'

She stretched out her hand for it, and began to sip. He picked up his own cup and saucer, watching her, telling himself that he was making the mistake which only a fool would make: he was believing her, although she must be lying. This set-up here must have been put on for his benefit, but—look at the evidence. Someone had come here, stripped her and bound her to the bed—a beastly experience for any woman. They had been pretty rough, too; the marks at her wrists and mouth showed that. Moreover, no one had come storming in to catch him in a compromising situation. If you believed evidence you believed evidence, not just that part of it which suited your own book.

She finished the tea, and when she spoke again her voice was much firmer and stronger.

'I know absolutely nothing about it, Mr. Dawlish,' she repeated. 'If my car was used I am terribly sorry.'

'So is Beresford.'

'Yes,' she said. 'Yes, I can understand how he feels and how you feel, but it wasn't Maurice. I'm as sure of that as I'm sitting here.'

'You can't be sure.'

'I can! He was in prison, I tell you.'

'I know all about that,' said Dawlish. 'He had a regular visitor too—the one person it would be easy to make arrangements with for a campaign like this.' He told Eileen Parish in rough sentences just what had happened, and all the time he tried to shock her into making some kind of an admission, but he failed.

'I can't help what has been done,' she insisted. 'I only know that it wasn't Maurice. I—oh, it's no use talking. You're determined not to believe me. You haven't even asked about the men who attacked me. They——'

'Later,' said Dawlish. 'Try making me believe you about Maurice Gorman.'

After a while she said rather breathlessly: 'It sounds so improbable—so corny. I was very fond of my sister and even more fond of Max—her son.' She paused, watching Dawlish as if to see that meant anything to him. He nodded. 'After my sister died, Maurice gave all his affection to Max. He didn't care for anyone else at all. I sometimes thought that he hated me because I was alive and Moira was dead, but I was able to help Max—Max was brought up in this house. Did you know that?'

'No.'

'Well, he was—from the time he was seven until the time he was seventeen, when he left school. Then Maurice took him away and they shared a flat in Mayfair. I always wished that he would come back here, I felt that there was something abnormal about the affection he gave to Max. It—it wasn't natural to be so utterly devoted.'

'It was a pity he didn't think of training his son differently,' Dawlish said.

'Yes, I know,' she agreed quietly. 'Mr. Dawlish, it wasn't until Max died that I knew what they had been doing. I had never realized that Maurice was a criminal. If I had I think I would have fought harder to get Max away from him. I—I simply had no idea. Everything was a most dreadful shock, but I was fond of Maurice, I loved Max, I owed my sister's memory something.' She stopped again, half-closed her eyes, and went on quietly, 'You see what I mean when I say that it sounds too corny?'

'Yes,' Dawlish said. It also sounded true, and perhaps the tone in which he spoke made her understand that he felt that, for a little of her tension eased as she went on:

'So I did everything I could for Maurice during the trial. After he was convicted, I went to see him at least four times a year, and after the first year I began to talk to him about you.' Now there was a curious intensity in the way the woman looked at Dawlish, as if she were willing him to believe her. 'That's why I remember everything about you and the Beresfords so clearly. I had to try to help Maurice, yet I knew how he hated you. He was—he was here for a day before the police caught him, and I thought he was going mad, because of Max's death.'

'Perhaps he did go mad,' Dawlish said.

'No,' she denied flatly. 'No, he was just terribly upset, but he was different afterwards. If he could have got at you or your wife, or the Beresfords that day he would have killed you, but he'd hurt his ankle—do you remember?—so he was fast to the house. I'm sure he would have tried to kill you if it hadn't been for that. It was after he had been sentenced, and he uttered those threats in court that I realized just how serious he was, how vital it was to change his mind.'

Dawlish said, more quietly, 'And how did you propose to set about that?'

'Mr. Dawlish, I can't help it if you refuse to believe me,' said Eileen Parish. 'I can't blame you either. If my car was used last night then I can understand how you feel, but I had only one purpose after Maurice had gone to Dartmoor. I had to make him change his whole attitude towards the future. I went down there regularly. I let him talk to me about it, hoping he would get it out of his system. I talked to him constantly. I told him that I liked you, your wife, and the Beresfords. I told him that you were only doing what you thought to be the right thing, and that he would be wickedly unfair to try to revenge himself. It wasn't any use rubbing in the fact that if he had trained Max differently, Max would never have died—there are some things you can't say. But I said everything I could. I even arranged help for him.'

'Help?' Dawlish echoed, startled.

He had forgotten the tea, forgotten the whisky and the brandy; for Eileen Parish was telling her story with remarkable persuasiveness, and it was difficult to disbelieve her. She stared into his eyes all the time, her gaze never shifting.

'Yes, help,' she repeated. 'I went to see the prison chaplain, and through him met several prison visitors, men who could talk Maurice's kind of language. I told them the problem, and asked them to help. I know they did. I'm sure that Maurice began to admit the folly of nursing hatred for you. It took a long time, but after about three years he no longer rejected everything I said, and towards the end of his time he told me that he'd been thinking of it day and night, and come to the conclusion that I was right. I—I am absolutely sure that he meant it.'

Dawlish could see three or four ex-convicts, men who had worked with Gorman on the Moor, who had broken stones with him, worked in the bakery and in the hessian sack shop, where he had spent much of his time. They had all said the same thing: that Gorman talked of nothing else but revenge. Not one of them had made the slightest reservation, but the last had talked to Gorman nearly three years ago. Certainly up to that time Gorman had been obsessed by his hatred.

He could have fooled his sister-in-law; or his outlook might have changed as she so obviously thought.

'You've got to believe me,' Eileen repeated, her voice much stronger. Her colour was better, too, although the patch where the plaster had stuck was still red and sore looking. The tiny globules of blood had dried into black spots. 'I'm sure that if you talk to Mr. Renfrew—the Prison Chaplain—or to Dr. Hislop, the Prison Visitor who helped most, they would say the same. Mr. Renfrew told me only two weeks ago that he was amazed by the change. He—but the letter's in the dressing-table!' Her eyes blazed. 'It's in the drawer on the right. Get it out, read it for yourself!'

Dawlish said, slowly, 'Yes, I will.' It was a relief to have an excuse to move, and he stood up slowly. The intensity of Eileen Parish's words and the depths of her feeling seemed unchallengeable, the possibility that she was lying to him seemed remote indeed. And no one had come, it seemed much less likely that this had been a frame-up, certainly not one of the obvious kind.

The woman wasn't lying about the letter. It was type-written, but the *Dear Miss Parish* was written in; so was the *Most sincerely yours* at the foot.


*Dear Miss Parish,*

*I understand that you already know that your brother-in-law will be released from Dartmoor because of his supreme act of bravery earlier in the year. I am very glad indeed about this. I think there is every reason to believe that this act of clemency and human understanding will be the final influence on Maurice Gorman. He will find it difficult and strange, of course, but few men who have left this place have been assured of such sympathy and understanding as you will be able to give.*

*There is very real cause to believe that Maurice Gorman will not revert to his past way of life, and every reason to believe that the great bitterness which he felt when he came here has been eased if not relieved completely.*

*And that—as well as a great deal more—has been due almost entirely to your patience and your steadfastness.*

*It has been a very great pleasure to know you and to try to help you.*

> *Most sincerely yours,*
> *Richard Renfrew*

As he read this, Dawlish was aware of the woman staring at him, and when he finished and glanced at her, great appeal seemd to glow in her eyes. He put the letter down, hesitated, and said with great deliberation:

'He believed you had succeeded, that's quite obvious. So did you. But you didn't succeed, Miss Parish.'

'I'm quite sure that we did,' she insisted. 'And—but what makes you feel so positive that Maurice is behind this—these awful crimes? Do you think prison's turned him into a fool? Surely only a fool would do this now. In a few months' time, or a few years' time, perhaps, but not *now*. He would realize that the police would suspect him from the beginning, the very thing he wants least would happen—he would be hounded wherever he went. He wants to come back here, live quietly for a few weeks, and then go abroad. He's planned it all, I've even made some arrangements for him. He—he's a completely reformed man, Mr. Dawlish, and I don't think that's for any moral reason. He knows that it's the only sensible thing for him, the only thing that will help him. You must believe it.'

Dawlish found himself thinking, 'I can believe it, too.'

Could he?

Would Ted?

What about the car, the hairs which were almost certainly from Joan's head, the fact that a tin plate of some kind had been wired on to the back of the old Austin?

Then Eileen said: 'And he wouldn't have done this to me, Mr. Dawlish. I'm absolutely positive about this: he would never have made me suffer an—an indignity like this.'

Wouldn't he? wondered Dawlish.

If she were right, there was so much to do, and so little hope of finding who was behind this campaign. It had been bad enough with a target, like Gorman; without one it was going to be a hundred times worse.

If she were right, who had taken the Austin? Who had come here and assaulted her? Who——

The sharp ringing of a bell broke across his thoughts. The door? Was the trap being sprung after all? The ringing went on, and he realized grimly that every ring of the telephone bell could fill him with tension. There was an instrument on a small table at the other side of the bed. Eileen hesitated. Dawlish said, 'I'll get it,' and went round to the other side while the bell was still ringing, hesitated in turn, and then lifted the receiver.

'Hallo,' he said.

'Hallo, Mr. Dawlish,' a man said, and laughed as if highly amused. 'Enjoying yourself?'

## CHAPTER X

## FACTS

DAWLISH caught his breath. Gorman's sister-in-law stared up, as if sensing what this call meant. Dawlish had a quick mental picture of the tramp's jaunty shoulders, then realized that he had been conditioned to react to such calls as this already; the man with the laughing voice was playing on his nerves with almost ludicrous ease. He, Dawlish, had been caught off balance with the first move, and hadn't yet recovered.

It was past time he did.

'Don't tell me you're at a loss for words again,' the caller said. 'I always understood that you were a most garrulous individual with great presence of mind.

Dawlish said, 'Really?' and chuckled. When he stopped, there was no immediate response, but Eileen was frowning as if surprised by the chuckle and the grin that went with it. Dawlish dropped on to the side of the bed, leaned back on one elbow, and spoke closer to the telephone. 'You may have misunderstood a lot of things, and you'll certainly have a lot of surprises coming to you. Have you any message for Miss Parish?'

'Er—yes, I have,' said the other man, but the laughter had gone from his voice; it was surprising how quickly a man could be put off his stroke. 'Tell her to look after her brother-in-law, he's a most important individual. And you——'

'I always look after myself,' Dawlish interrupted. 'Don't worry about me for a moment. I'll be seeing you.' He rang off before the other man could speak again, banging the receiver down, and there was more brightness in his voice when he spoke to Eileen. 'Do you know of a man who laughs when he talks?'

She looked puzzled.

'So you don't,' Dawlish said. 'He's the joker I told you about, the one who telephoned from Exeter. He knew that I was likely to be here, too.' He rubbed the broken bridge of his nose again, and went on: 'I don't know how well you think you worked on your brother-in-law, but I know one thing. If he isn't behind all this, he's likely to be blamed for it. You are, too. Evidence is the key factor, and all the evidence so far points to you.'

She didn't answer.

Dawlish asked, 'How do you feel now?'

'I'm much better,' she said. 'At least I have to thank you for that.' She wasn't really thinking about what she was saying, something else was developing in her mind. She soon explained. 'Mr. Dawlish, you may try to ignore the fact, but two men attacked me about two hours before you came. I had never seen either of them before. They had scarves on their faces, but one scarf slipped and I think I would know the man again from the glimpse I had of him.'

'If you didn't see them, how do you know they were strangers?' asked Dawlish, quietly.

'I didn't recognize their voices.'

'Point to you,' Dawlish said. 'Were they rough?'

'Very.'

'Did they say anything?'

'Not really,' she answered. 'They talked between themselves, and when I tried to resist they told me that——' she broke off.

'Let's have it,' Dawlish urged. 'I'm ready for this fairy story now.'

She said, flushing: 'When are you going to realize that I am telling the truth? The men said that I ought to think myself lucky that they didn't rape me. They didn't exactly put it in those words, but made it very clear.'

'Nice pair,' said Dawlish, and wondered if a woman who was lying to him would have flushed as she did then; whether the colour in her cheeks was not the surest indication yet that she had told the absolute truth. 'Did they say anything else? Why they were doing it, for instance?'

'No.'

'Did you let them in?'

She didn't answer; that was the first time she had hesitated and the first time she gave the impression that she would like to keep something back.

'Did you?'

'No,' she answered at last. They got in with a key. I was getting ready to go out—sitting on that stool. I saw the door open, that was the first time I realized that anything was wrong. They were in the room almost before I could move, and——' she gulped, and her cheeks turned fiery red. 'One of them held my arms behind while the other pulled off my clothes.' She glanced at the flimsy oddments of clothing opposite the door, and again Dawlish felt that no woman could pretend to be so affected. The very placing of the clothes by the door, so that the first person who came in would see them, fitted in perfectly with all she said had happened. The two men had played it rough; they had threatened but had not really harmed her.

They had been very sure of themselves.

How could they have been so confident that he would come here?

It was a fair guess, Dawlish argued with himself. Anyone who knew Dawlish would know that he was likely to work on his own. He was bound to learn about the sister-in-law's visits to Dartmoor. There was a very good chance that he would want to see Eileen Parish ahead of the police. It was really a matter of intelligent guesswork, and Dawlish himself was guessing. Only one thing was positive. This hate campaign was being directed with acute intelligence, and all the moves had been planned well in advance. At least he could take more risks now that Felicity was safely out of the way.

Dawlish did not realize that it was almost the first time he had given conscious thought to Felicity since he had walked out of Trivett's room. He did realize that he had been silent for a long time, but Gorman's sister-in-law made no attempt to prompt him. He could not prove that she was lying, and it might be wise to appear to believe her.

'I'm probably a lunatic,' he said, 'but I'm beginning to doubt if you knew anything about the attack or the murder.'

'I don't know anything,' Eileen Parish insisted, and then startled him by adding: 'But I want to, Mr. Dawlish. I'm just beginning to realize what you mean when you say that Maurice is likely to be blamed for it. This is obviously why the attacks on you and the Beresfords were timed now, to

make sure you and the police suspect my brother-in-law.'
She was looking at him very straightly, and he had a strong
feeling that he would be shaken by whatever she said next;
her intent showed in the way she looked, in a momentary
hesitation, in an involuntary movement of her hands.
Although the sheet dropped from her shoulder again,
Dawlish did not really notice it. 'Mr. Dawlish, I believe that
my brother-in-law wants to forget his old life. I'm quite sure
that he doesn't want to risk going back to prison. He will need
help desperately now. Will you do all you can to help him?'

\* \* \* \* \*

Was she naïve to a point of real simplicity? Was she simply
earnest? Or was she fooling him? It was easy to believe the
last: appealing to him to help Gorman would have a sharp
edge of malicious wit—the same kind of mockery as in the
laughter of the man of the telephone. Her question did more
to make Dawlish doubt the truth of her story than anything
else; suddenly she seemed to be going too far.

Did she realize it?

She said: 'And it would serve your interest too, you can't
make any mistake about that. If Maurice is being framed—
isn't that the word?'

'It could be,' Dawlish agreed dryly.

'If someone is trying to make you suspect him, obviously
the same people are working against you, and the same
people killed Mrs. Beresford,' declared Eileen Parish.

There was clear and undeniable logic, and it seemed to
round off everything that had happened here a little too
smoothly. Fresh questions crowded Dawlish's mind, both for
and against her. If she were involved, would she have allowed
her car to be used? the faking of an attack was understand-
able and easy to accept, and the men hadn't really harmed
her; any woman would soon recover from the indignity. But
the car . . .

'I know it's a new idea,' Eileen said, 'but don't refuse to
help just because of that. Think about it.'

Dawlish found himself chuckling.

'All right,' he said. 'Judgment postponed. Let's have a look
at a few facts. The police will soon be here. They'll establish
these facts—about the car and certain other things. They
won't be as willing as I am to believe that you might have
worked a miracle with your brother-in-law. You might find

yourself held on suspicion of complicity in Mrs. Beresford's murder. In fact, you almost certainly will.'

Apparently she hadn't thought of that, and if she were criminally inclined, or had any training in crime, surely she would have realized the possibility from the beginning. That was how his thoughts veered—now towards her and now away from her, changing minute by minute.

There was another thing.

She was quite a woman. Even in spite of the patches at her lips, she was easy to look at, and she had most beautiful eyes and a most beautiful body. She could have used it, to distract him. Everything had been perfectly set for a seduction scene, and she hadn't even attempted to take advantage of it. If she had been setting out to fool him, would she have missed that chance?

The truth was that he didn't know.

'If—if I'm arrested, I can't help it,' she said, after a pause. 'I would be desperately sorry because I think Maurice will need me here, but if I can't help myself——' she broke off, with a rueful shrug. 'I'm not planning to run away, if that's what you mean. I was out from half past three yesterday afternoon until nearly ten o'clock last night, and I didn't take the car because it's hopeless to try to park in the West End. That is the simple truth, Mr. Dawlish.'

Dawlish said briskly: 'Right! Don't try to run away. I'll try to make sure that the police don't act too fast, whatever they think. Mind answering a few personal questions?'

'I have no objections at all.'

'Whose house is this?'

'Mine,' she answered, promptly. 'It was my parents,' and was left to me—my sister died a few months before my parents, so I inherited everything. The house, the car and over thirty thousand pounds, Mr. Dawlish. I lead a very lazy life. I like travelling but don't much like driving, that's why I've never bought a more modern car. I've everything I could possibly need.'

'How old are you?'

'I am thirty-five.'

That looked about right, thought Dawlish; five years younger than Felicity or Joan. She showed no resentment or hesitation at the question, in some ways she was a most remarkable woman.

'And you don't think you need a husband?' Dawlish demanded, almost brutally.

Eileen hesitated, frowning and he wondered whether he had gone too far, but she still showed no resentment when she said:

'I was engaged ten years ago and my fiance was killed in a road accident. You are wrong in what you're thinking, Mr. Dawlish. I am not in love with Maurice, and I never have been. Moira—my sister—always used to say that I had been cursed with a Puritan conscience, and I suppose there is something in that. If I think it is my duty to take a certain course of action, I take it. Trying to help Maurice is an obligation for a very happy childhood and happy memories of my sister. That is the simple truth.'

That was the moment when Dawlish felt virtually convinced that whatever the truth about Gorman, she was telling the truth about herself.

Dawlish said, 'All right, we'll see,' and lifted the telephone. He dialled Whitehall 1212, and asked for Trivett, who came on the line almost at once. In short, brisk sentences Dawlish told him exactly what had happened and what he had found, and his description of the attack on Eileen Parish was almost clinical in its clarity. When he had finished the explanation, he went on:

'If I were you, Bill, I'd leave the Parish woman alone for a while, and see what happens now. There's a good fifty-fifty chance that she's telling the truth. That's if you don't mind a suggestion!'

'You're probably right,' Trivett conceded. 'I'll send a team over right away to see the car and the garage, and look over the house. Want them to try to shake the woman's story?'

'Yes. How's Felicity?'

'As safe as houses,' Trivett answered. 'Don't worry about her.' He rang off, leaving Dawlish reassured at least about Felicity.

Eileen Parish stretched out an arm, long, rounded and lovely, touched Dawlish's hand and said:

'Thank you again.'

*Was* she too naïve? Dawlish looked at her steadily, and his gaze dropped to her bosom. She drew the sheet up, rather hastily, and quite suddenly he grinned and stood up.

'It's time you became what the old-fashioned call respectable, and put some clothes on. I'll be back in ten minutes.' He turned towards the door, and as he reached it heard a car pulling up nearby. Trivett couldn't have a car here yet, could he? He glanced at the window, had a swift picture of Eileen

Parish sitting up in bed with the sheet clutched in both hands high, up to her neck, and looking quite lovely.

The car stopped. By the time he was half-way down the stairs, a door slammed. He reached the front room and hurried to the window, just in time to see a taxi moving off, and a man of medium height, looking very bronzed and fit and lean, walking towards the house with a small case in his right hand. He was staring at the front door with great intensity.

The neighbour across the road was still at her window; would she also recognize this man?

Maurice Gorman passed out of Dawlish's sight, and a moment later there was a ring at the front-door bell.

## CHAPTER XI

## CHANGED MAN?

THE bell had hardly stopped ringing before Dawlish was at the door. He moved on his toes and made no sound except for a creaking board, as he went up the stairs. The bell did not ring again, and there was a scraping of a key being turned in the lock. Dawlish swung round the bend in the banister rail, and thrust himself into the bedroom. Eileen was standing by the side of the bed, without a stitch on, turning round to stare at him, not even a sheet handy for modesty's sake.

Dawlish said softly: It's Gorman. Put on a dressing-gown, go and let him in, let him do the talking. If you warn him I'm here, I'll make the police take the pair of you to the Yard; they'll do it gladly. Got that?'

'Ye—yes,' she whispered.

'Get a move on,' Dawlish urged, turned round, and looked back at her over his shoulder; she was already moving towards the wardrobe, one hand outstretched. 'Tell him you locked yourself in because you were scared. Tell him you managed to use a pair of scissors.'

'All right,' Eileen said huskily.

The bell rang again.

Dawlish stepped on to the landing. Opposite the main bedroom door was a small cupboard, and he could step inside and hide there with a door ajar. He heard the wardrobe door open, followed by a rustling sound, and another sound he hadn't expected. He thought that a window was being thrust

64

up, and peered into the bedroom. The woman was standing at the window, a red dressing-gown round her, and she leaned out. Her words floated back to him.

'*Who is it?*'

She had a needle-quick mind, and was quite capable of fooling him or anyone. He did not hear the response, but heard her gasp as if astounded:

'*Maurice!*' There was a pause, before she added: 'I won't be a minute. I've got to put something on.' She turned away from the window and Dawlish backed into his hiding place. She didn't see him there, but looked about the landing as she came out a minute later, the quilted gown draping almost to her ankles, and wearing pink slippers. He watched her through the slightly open door. She moved very well, in spite of what had happened, and was wearing mules; her heels looked pink and rosy every time she took a step. She hesitated at the top of the stairs, and Dawlish called:

'Don't say a word about me.'

'I won't,' she promised, and added as if she meant to make sure that he believed her: 'I need your help, I won't let you down.'

The she moved towards the hall, in a curious kind of floating motion. Dawlish hardly heard a sound of her footsteps, but the drawing of the bolts and moving of the chain sounded sharp and clear. The door opened. Dawlish crept to the head of the stairs, stood where he could not be seen until the others were half-way along the hall, and listened intently.

'Hallo, Maurice,' Eileen greeted. 'It's good to have you home.' Gorman didn't respond, and Dawlish wondered if she was adding something in a whisper, but he did not hear even a sibilant, until she went on: 'You said you wouldn't be here until tonight.'

'I caught an earlier train,' Gorman said.

Dawlish remembered his voice well—sharp and incisive, the voice of a man of good education; he had been to one of the middle-grade public schools. He had always had an air with him, and a convincing manner; that was what had made him such a success with old ladies he had planned to swindle.

'Why have you barred and bolted yourself in?' he asked in a casual way. 'I've seen enough locked doors to last me a lifetime.'

That was the kind of thing a man would say if he really meant to take no risks.

'I—I'll tell you in a minute,' Eileen said. 'I had—I had a rather nasty experience, Maurice. But you'll be tired after the journey. Let's go and make a cup of tea.'

After another pause, Gorman said:

'What kind of nasty experience? I want to know now, Eileen. I've had a bad enough day as it is.'

Eileen caught her breath.

'*Bad?*'

'I was questioned by the police at Exeter. Two more got on my train at Salisbury, and another two were waiting at Waterloo,' Gorman said, harshly. 'That's what happens when you come out of prison. Your friends Renfrew and Hislop and their smooth talk didn't mean a thing. The police aren't going to give me a chance to forget the past.' There was another pause, and in it Dawlish moved so that he could just see the pair. They were standing a yard apart, and nothing in their manner suggested that they were fond of each other, or that they had kissed. In fact there seemed a kind of restraint between them.

'It's so unfair!' Eileen exclaimed.

'You'll soon learn how vindictive the police are,' Gorman said bitterly. 'Oh, I don't want to hurt your feelings. I know you've done everything anyone could and you even had me fooled. I thought they would at least watch me from a distance.'

'What—what did they want to know?'

'They asked me about some of the men who were in Dartmoor with me, God knows why. But we can't stand here. I could do with that cup of tea, it's been a lousy journey and there was no heat on that blasted train.' Gorman stooped to pick up his case, and Eileen turned. Dawlish backed out of sight, while first the woman and the man walked past the foot of the stairs and to the kitchen. Dawlish went down the stairs, sliding on the banisters and landing on his toes. The kitchen-door was half-closed, and he could hear the others moving about. There was the sound of running water, too. Some tea things were upstairs and there was a chance that Gorman would notice that. Dawlish was trying to reconcile what Gorman was saying with everything he knew about the man, and with what had happened to Joan and to him.

'Now, what's this about a nasty experience?' Gorman demanded.

'Maurice, I——'

'I suppose the police have been here too. Is that it?' Gorman guessed, and there was hardness and bitterness in his voice. 'If they have, I——'

'Maurice, you can't blame the police for this!'

'That's enough of that,' Gorman rasped. 'I can take so much do-gooding from you, but there's a limit. The police didn't give me even two hours' peace. That's the truth about it—not a couple of hours. God knows what they think I've been able to do on the Moor. God knows why I haven't rotted in that bloody place, and . . .' There was a moment's hesitation and then a softening in his tone. 'I probably would have, but for you. I'm not ungrateful, Eileen, but I can't take any more moralizing. I had a bellyfull from Renfrew yesterday, and plenty from the Governor. Let's cut it out. There's no reason at all why the police shouldn't give me a chance to settle down without pestering me.'

'Maurice,' Eileen said, 'Ted Beresford's wife was murdered last night.'

After she had said that the only sound was the faint hissing of the electric kettle. Dawlish wished that he could see Gorman's face, and crept closer to the door, but the woman was towards it. He could see her face, turned slightly away from him, looking very composed, although pale; the red patch at her lips had faded to a slight pink, and she had found time to wipe off those little dots of dried blood.

Then Gorman said, as if in horror, '*No.*' Dawlish saw him put out a hand, as if he wanted support; then saw him move forward towards the kitchen table and lean against it. He didn't take his gaze away from the woman. Dawlish saw his side face, and it seemed certain that the man was really shocked. The hissing of the kettle seemed to make the tension greater.

Gorman repeated: 'Oh, God! But——' His eyes blazed. *Last* night? If it happened last night, they can't suspect me!'

'They think you might be working with someone else,' Eileen answered flatly.

Gorman said, stupidly. 'They can't be so crazy, they can't ——' and then broke off as if suddenly understanding why he could be suspected. He moistened his lips. 'I get it now. They questioned me about three men who hate Dawlish's guts. I get it all right. They think I'm in a conspiracy to——' He broke off again, and then thwacked a clenched fist into an open palm. 'What do they think I am? A lunatic? It I were going to start reprisals against Dawlish, would I do it now? Would

I choose the very time I know I'd be suspected? I haven't even had time to breathe!'

'That's what I told——' Eileen began, and then broke off. 'I must make the tea, the kettle's boiling its head off.' She turned to go, but Gorman shot out a hand and clutched her wrist; there was restrained violence in the way he pulled her towards him.

'Who did you talk to? Come on, let me know the worst. What's all this about a nasty experience?' He was closer to her now and thrusting his face forward, as if trying to frighten her into answering.

'Let me go, Maurice,' Eileen said, quite calmly. 'I'll tell you as soon as I've switched the kettle off.' When he didn't release her, she spoke more sharply, 'Maurice, don't be silly.'

It was quite something for Gorman to be treated rather like a child who was misbehaving, to see the way he obeyed. Eileen Parish's composure did not change, and she turned away. Dawlish could not see what happened, but the kettle stopped boiling, and a rattle of cups and saucers followed. Gorman moved to the far end of the kitchen, out of sight.

'Eileen, tell me what happened.'

'All right, Maurice,' she said. 'But you ought to sit down.' She waited until he did so, and then began to talk in her rational way, telling about the visit from the two men, describing exactly what had happened in a manner so dispassionate that it seemed to add to the horror of the incident, and to make its beastliness worse. She finished quite suddenly:

'And that's all I can tell you, Maurice.'

Gorman didn't answer.

She poured out tea, and Dawlish heard the gurgling in the cups. Still Gorman didn't speak. There was a rustle of movement, and Eileen said: 'I must get some aspirins. I've a wicked headache,' and moved towards the door. She was coming to see if Dawlish was near, of course, to ask what she should say next. The door opened. Dawlish was pressed against one wall, and Eileen saw him at once, but Gorman was staring straight ahead of him as if struck dumb and motionless.

'Tell him the rest,' Dawlish whispered.

Eileen nodded, then beckoned him. She went briskly up the stairs, and the backs of the mules kept slapping the bottoms of her feet; she made much more noise than Dawlish as he followed her. They reached the landing, as she went towards the bathroom, Eileen said in a very low-pitched voice:

'Surely you can see that it's a terrible shock to him. You must help him.'

'If he knows nothing about the murder, I'll help him,' Dawlish promised.

She turned and faced him. Her eyes were hardly bloodshot at all now, and their brown beauty glowed. She took his arms and gripped them tightly as she said:

'You've got to. If the wrong thing happens now, he won't ever recover. You've got to find out who's doing this, *quickly*.'


CHAPTER XII

## FACE TO FACE

FIVE minutes afterwards Eileen had told Gorman everything about Dawlish's visit, what he had said, what he had done, what he had promised. Gorman hardly said a word, but sat at the kitchen table, occasionally sipping his tea. Eileen had left the door ajar so that Dawlish could see through without being seen. There was a kind of hopelessness in Gorman's bearing and in his voice, almost as convincing as the woman's manner.

There was one thing to remember, Dawlish warned himself. The man with the laughing voice had telephoned, and knew that he was here. Gorman might have met that man, or more likely, might have had a message from him, and therefore know that Dawlish had come. This could be a skilfully put up job. Gorman was undoubtedly a clever man, and might have been planning the form of his revenge for years. He might have rehearsed every possible scene in any conceivable situation, too. If Eileen Parish was all she seemed to be, Gorman would have to make her believe in him, would have to talk to her as he was doing.

So this could be an act on Gorman's part.

'And the police are coming soon,' Eileen went on. 'That—that's why I was so shocked when you came early, Maurice. I didn't want you to run into them, and I'd no idea that you'd already seen them. Maurice . . .' when the man didn't respond, Eileen went on more sharply: 'Maurice, do you know who is doing this? Can you guess? Can you help the police?'

'Oh, no,' said Gorman, brusquely. 'There are a lot of things I will do, but I won't help the police. Dawlish is getting what's been coming to him for a long time. If it hadn't been for you, I would have been ready to have a go at him myself. You and Renfrew persuaded me that it wasn't any use planning revenge, but you didn't make me like Dawlish. I hate his guts. If it weren't for one thing, I'd go out and wave a flag—the more Dawlish and lousy friends suffer, the better I'll like it.'

Dawlish wondered what the woman was thinking, knowing that he was listening to this.

She asked, 'What is that one thing, Maurice?'

'That the police will think I'm playing a part in it,' Gorman answered, and added visciously: 'And they'll fake some evidence, too. Take it from me, they'll find a way to get me inside again, and before I know where I am I'll be back on the Moor. I'm only out on sufferance, they can send me back any time they want to.' Dawlish saw him clenching his hands tightly, saw the way his chin was thrust forward, saw the glitter in his eyes. 'Don't ask me to help Dawlish or the police.'

'It's the only way you can help yourself,' Eileen argued, stubbornly.

Dawlish pushed the door open wider, and stepped inside. Gorman saw the first movement out of the corner of his eye, and turned his head sharply; when Dawlish appeared, he half-rose from the table, hands pressing heavily against it, peering up. In that moment he was surprisingly like the son who had died. Dartmoor had made him thinner, perhaps that was one of the reasons for the resemblance; he had been running to fat. Dawlish stepped further in. Eileen dropped into a chair, as if at last her nerves were giving way.

Gorman breathed very harshly.

Dawlish said, 'It looks to me as if your old pals are framing you, Gorman.' When the man didn't answer, Dawlish moved further forward, and went on very easily. 'When did you give up the idea of trying to cut my throat?'

Gorman still didn't answer.

Dawlish waited, his mind working very fast, checking everything he could against the tactics which seemed most likely to bring results. If Gorman thought that he, Dawlish, believed in his change of heart, he might be lured into making a mistake. The vital thing was not to close his mind to anything, neither to the possibility of a Gorman who had given up evil intent, nor to the possibility that Gorman had planned

70

all this with Machiavellian devilry. The man was looking up at him from under his brows, still breathing through his lips, so softly that he hardly seemed to be breathing at all.

'*For goodness' sake don't just stand there!*' Eileen burst out.

Gorman gulped, moved his chair back with his legs and stood upright. He glanced at his sister-in-law, then stared at Dawlish again.

He said: 'Let's get one thing clear, Dawlish. I hate your guts. If it weren't for you my son would be alive today. You killed him as surely as if you'd stuck a knife into him. There isn't a thing that would make me help you. If someone else is after you, that's all right with me. If I'm caught in the middle of the war, that's all right with me, too. I've spent seven years on the Moor, and in every one of those years I learned how to hate you more. If I knew who had killed Beresford's wife, if I knew who was going to kill you, I wouldn't breathe a word. I'd rather hang. Don't think my sister-in-law can make me change my mind, either. No one can. I wouldn't lift a finger to help you, I wouldn't throw you a piece of straw if you were drowning. And I hope they kill you. I hope they——'

'*Don't say it!*' Eileen shouted, and sprang forward. 'You fool, you don't realize what you're doing! Dawlish can help you. It's as vital to him as it is to you. Don't say these things!'

'I hope they get your wife first and you afterwards,' Gorman said, and at last he looked at his sister-in-law. 'Who has to get out? Dawlish or me? I'm not going to stay here another five minutes while he's here.'

* * * * *

Dawlish thought, he hasn't changed at all. He watched the man and woman staring, almost glaring, at each other. He did not think he had anything more to learn here, and there was no point in staying for the sake of it. The police would soon arrive; it must be half an hour or more since he had telephoned them. He wished that there were some way he could help the woman, wished he could make some comment to sting Gorman, but that would not be easy. He felt further away than ever from a solution to the problem; the meeting which should have told him so much had told him practically nothing.

He said: 'They won't get me or my wife, Gorman, and you won't, either. Everyone involved in this murder will be caught before the week's out. Make sure your friends know that.' He looked at Eileen. 'The police will be here soon. If he

71

talks to them like he's talked to me, they'll take him back with them, and they'll also take you.'

He nodded to her, swung round and strode towards the door. It was now sagging open a little, because of the broken lock. He pulled it wider, and a blast of cold evening air came in. He started when he saw a big man standing on the doorstep. His heart seemed to turn over, he thrust his hands outwards as if to fend of an attack; but almost on the instant, he realized that this was a man from the Yard.

It was Detective-Sergeant Plummer.

'Sorry sir,' Plummer said. 'I heard you talking and I thought it better to keep away until you'd finished.' When Dawlish didn't answer, the Yard man went on, 'He doesn't seem to have changed much, does he?'

'No,' Dawlish said. 'Who else is here?'

'Chief Inspector Gilson's round the back, having a look at the car,' Plummer answered. 'We saw you through the kitchen window, that's why we didn't knock or ring. Superintendent Trivett gave strict instructions that you were to be given all possible facilities.'

'Ah,' said Dawlish. 'Fine. Thanks.' He took out the insulation tape, and handed it to Plummer. 'This might be the tape used on that broken telephone wire. I brought it away from the garage here. I'll be in touch. Thanks.' He stepped forward, and Plummer moved to one side. Dawlish did not glance round, but went straight to the Allard. It was quite dark; he had not realized how dark when he had been in the kitchen. Two teenage boys were admiring the Allard, and moved away rather sheepishly when he reached it. He found a smile for them, and said, 'If you're crazy enough, she'll do a hundred and twenty.' He got in, started the engine, and drove off as if he meant to do a hundred and twenty before he reached the corner. He waved to the youths, and the trifling incident did a little to take the oppressiveness of the burden off his mind. He slowed down. Two policemen were at the corner, and just round it there were two police cars.

Trivett was being very good.

Dawlish drove more slowly through the thickening traffic. There was a heavy mist which seemed to be thickening, too, as if the sunshine was going to be avenged by a night of fog. He kept glancing in his driving mirror, but no one followed him. He reached the mews, to find a uniformed constable on duty outside. The flat was in darkness. He wondered how long Beresford would be, and told himself that he would probably stay in Oxford most of the evening; it was easy to say that one wouldn't stay long with a bereaved mother, a very different matter to leave her.

Dawlish went up the four steps of the flat, thinking bleakly of Felicity. The last thing he wanted to do was to spend any time here on his own; this was not a good time for brooding. Then he saw the box of groceries at the door; he almost stumbled over them because it was very dark just here, the only light in the mews being misted with the fog. He stared down, remembering that Ted had said there was little food in, that he'd left the ordering to Joan.

Ted hadn't ordered this.

He called, 'Come here one of you, will you?' and a plain-clothes man came hurrying. 'Who delivered this?' There was sharpness in his manner which obviously startled the man.

'Merrow and Webb's, sir.'

'Sure?'

'Positive.'

'Did you recognize the driver?'

'No, sir, but it was one of their usual vans—striped green and black, vertically. If I hadn't been sure I wouldn't have let them leave it. The man had Mrs. Beresford's account book, too—I insisted on seeing that.'

'Ah,' said Dawlish. 'Yes, quite right. Thanks.' He peered down at the box. 'Get the torch from my car, will you? I'd like this checked closely before we take any chances.'

'I've a flash-light, sir.'

'Thanks,' said Dawlish. A beam of light shot out, misty against the fog and yet shining vividly enough on the packed groceries. There was butter, lard, bacon and cheese on top, a thick piece of cardboard separating them from soap and washing powder, and beneath the provisions there were the packed goods. 'Better lift them out one by one,' Dawlish said, and yet hesitated to do so, for this might be another booby-trap. Would it be anything which would explode when subjected to sudden movement? That wasn't likely, surely; if it were another inflammable sachet of nitro-glycerine, it would almost certainly have exploded in the van, and never got this far.

So any explosive in the box would probably be set with a time fuse. The packet goods should be all right.

Or would they be?

'It *looks* all right, sir,' the plain-clothes man commented.

'Yes,' agreed Dawlish. 'Yes.' He began to think: 'If it were a nitro sachet where could it be put safely?' and the answer came almost at once: 'In sugar or some other powder which could be packed round it tightly and so lessen the risk of concussion and an explosion.' In the house, sugar would be emptied into a dish, possibly into a jar, or spooned out quite vigorously. Tea would be emptied, too, and flour might be. So the flour and the sugar wanted examining first. They were in sealed bags, and the flour-bag was soft and easy to press in. He examined the seal at the top, and felt fairly sure that it had not been tampered with. He turned to the sugar, and the plain-clothes man said:

'That packet looks as if it's been opened once, sir.'

'Yes,' said Dawlish. 'Yes, Stuck down carelessly, too. Move back a bit, will you?'

'Excuse *me*, sir,' said the plain-clothes man, firmly. 'My instructions are to take all necessary steps to save you from any kind of attack. This is my job. And I let them put it here, anyhow.' It was obvious that he also believed the worst, and Dawlish let him do what he wanted, backing away only a little. The man's lean fingers moved briskly, he showed no signs of nervousness, and Dawlish wasn't surprised when he went on: 'I've done one or two bomb disposal jobs in my time, this one is chicken feed.' He poked two fingers down into the granulated sugar, then stopped moving. He glanced up at Dawlish and said, 'Summat here.' He straightened up, and added: 'Mind spreading that newspaper out on the step for me, sir? No need to make a mess.' He waited until Dawlish had taken a newspaper and laid it out, then began to pour a trickle of sugar from the packet with extreme care. Dawlish held the torch, and was the first to see the corner of something small and dark show against the white crystals.

'Hold it!'

'I'll be careful, sir.' The man shook a little more sugar out, until the edge of a shiny glass container, the same shape as the sachet like those Dawlish had seen before, showed clearly.

'My God, they certainly mean to get you!' the plain-clothes man said.

## CHAPTER XIII

## EVIDENCE

THERE was nothing else dangerous in the groceries, but the brittle glass container did contain nitro-glycerine.

By the time that was known for certain the police had been to the Piccadilly head office of Merrow and Webb, and talked to the order clerk and the delivery-van driver. The order had been telephoned by a man a little after two o'clock, and a special request had been made for delivery that afternoon. It had been just in time for the normal delivery, and the mews had been the seventh stop of the van's schedule. There had therefore been six opportunities for someone to tamper with the orders for the Beresfords.

Dawlish was at the Yard about six o'clock.

'They probably bought the sugar somewhere else, put the nitro in it, and simply substituted that packet for one in the box,' Trivett reasoned. 'It wouldn't take half a minute, and there would be no danger until the sugar was emptied out of the bag into a tin or a jar. That brittle glass would easily break, and there would be sufficient motion to set it off.'

Dawlish didn't speak.

'We've checked the sugar container, but the only prints on it are a store clerk's,' Trivett went on. 'We can't get any help from that. We might get some from the insulation tape you found, though. There was a smooth patch, and it shows part of a fingerprint. It will need working on and enlarging before we can check to see if it's anyone with a record.'

'Hurry,' urged Dawlish. 'Was the tape used on the telephone wire taken from the roll I found in the garage?'

'Yes.'

'Well, well.'

'The tyre-prints on that Austin are identical with the prints found near the river at Chiswick,' Trivett went on, 'and scratches on the bumper on the Austin are new, almost certainly made by the wire which fastened on the hackney carriage plate. There isn't any doubt at all that Joan was taken away in Eileen Parish's car.'

Dawlish didn't speak.

'We found some hairs—Joan's hairs—in the back of the car,' Trivett added, his voice empty of feeling. 'They were on the floor, on the seat, and some were tucked down at the back of the seat. You can be sure that her head was against that seat at some time or other.' He hesitated, and had to make himself go on to say,' 'She was probably strangled while lying back in the car.'

'Yes,' Dawlish said, stonily. 'Find anything else at Mountjoy Street?' ...

'No. The only prints are those of Eileen Parish, a few of Gorman's, a daily woman's, and some you left. The sister-in-law says the men who attacked her had some cloth on their fingers—tape, of course.'

Trivett hesitated before asking slowly: 'What do you feel about Eileen Parish, Pat? Do you think she is in it, and that she allowed hereself to be assaulted? No positive injury resulted—she wasn't molested, as we say. It could be part of an elaborate frame.'

'I know.'

'But you don't think so.'

'I wouldn't go halfway towards saying that,' Dawlish declared. 'I think the woman's probably in the clear, but——' he broke off. 'I'm not going to commit myself to any other opinion yet. What did your chaps say?'

'They were well impressed by her,' Trivett admitted, 'and they thought that Gorman was too vicious about you to be putting up an act. He told them what he told you: he wouldn't lift a finger to help, and hoped you got what was coming to you. I could have held him, as what he said could be stretched into threats and menaces, but I let him go. He's being closely followed and the house is being watched.'

'He won't make any overt move,' Dawlish declared. He hesitated, pressed a hand against his forehead, and went on: 'I've a hell of a headache, blast it. So all we've really got are those fingerprints and the fact that Eileen Parish's Austin was used.'

'Yes.'

'Not much,' Dawlish complained. 'Not half enough. I've been doing some thinking, too. Of all the men who told the world what they would do to me when they got out, I'd say there were two who might have meant what they said.'

'Who?'

'Johnny Chalke and Fred Holsen.'

'We'd wondered about that pair, too,' said Trivett. 'They were both on the Moor, they often worked in the same stone-breaking gang as Gorman, and the three of them could have worked together. Chalke and Holsen knew each other, although they were in for different crimes. They're both well fixed—they salted plenty of money away before they were sent down. Chalke's married, Holsen has a kind of semi-permanent liaison with a young Frenchwoman. They've been going straight for at least six months as far as we know, and they've no reason not to continue to go straight—but they're the type who would lay on a job like this, and carry it out for revenge, provided they weren't taking too much risk.'

Dawlish said, heavily, 'You mean, provided they had someone to take the rap for them.'

'Yes.'

'Like Gorman.'

'Yes.'

'What are you doing about them?'

'I'm having them both checked, trying to find out if either of them sent anyone to Exeter yesterday, or whether any of their associates corresponds with the description of your tramp. But the tramp could have worn a wig, and if he shaved——'

'I'd recognize him,' Dawlish declared. 'The trouble will be getting someone else to recognize him from my description. No more news from Haslemere?'

'No.'

Dawlish said, 'I wonder what time Ted will be back.'

'I shouldn't expect him tonight,' Trivett advised. 'I had a word with the Oxford Police just before you arrived, and they tell me that Joan's mother is in a pretty bad way—first hysterical, then in a state of collapse. And Ted is going to stay there if Joan's sister has anything to do with it. I asked the Oxford chaps to get a local doctor to give him a shot of morphia. He'll crack up if he doesn't get some rest.' Trivett looked hard into Dawlish's eyes, and went on, 'And you must take it easy, you look as if the top of your head will blow off.'

'That's how I feel,' said Dawlish. 'I'll get back to the flat.' He went to the door, and half turned. 'How's Fel?'

'Doing fine!'

'Thanks,' said Dawlish, quietly.

Trivett walked with him to the lift, then left him on his own. He went down, nodded to men on duty at the main hall, and went out into the foggy night. The acrid sharpness of smog stung his nostrils, and it could be both a danger and a help. At least no one could follow him easily, but the risk of being attacked by a man leaping out of the fog was real enough, although only likely if he went to places which he was known to visit.

His club, for instance—or Tim Jeremy's flat. It was a pity that Tim was away, a talk with him would make a world of difference.

Dawlish pressed his hand against his forehead again. He felt sick with the headache, and had seldom known a worse one. Then he realized that apart from a sandwich at lunch-time, he hadn't eaten all day; he was famished. At his club he could get a steak which would soon put that right.

Ought he to go to his club?

'No,' he said softly, in the murky night. 'No, I'd better keep away.' The ugly truth was that danger might strike at any time, might come as casually as out of a two-pound packet of sugar.

He walked with long strides along Whitehall, seeing shape-less figures appearing out of the murk, and vanishing. There was a glow of light above his head at the street lamps. Buses and a few private cars were crawling; if this fog worsened, traffic would be at a standstill. He watched every figure approaching, and kept looking over his shoulder. He kept thinking of a vague fingerprint on the insulation tape, too, which hadn't been identified, of a man with laughter in his voice, of Johnny Chalke and Fred Holsen.

If they were involved, they would be expecting a visit from him, just as they had expected him to go to Mountjoy Street. Trivett hadn't told him where they lived, which meant that Trivett did not want him to go to either place on his own.

Dawlish reached Trafalgar Square, crossed it with a small crowd at the lights, saw about a dozen people bearing down on him from the other side of the road; any one of them might be coming for him. He prepared himself for a collision but there was none. Half—most—of his fears were imagin-ary. He walked along by St. Martin-in-the-Fields and then into St. Martin's Lane, turned into a small restaurant where the steaks were renowned, ordered a big fillet with onion soup to start with. He hadn't realized how hungry he was. He piled butter on to crisp rolls, drank a pint of light ale, showered Parmesan cheese into the soup, demolished the steak and chipped potatoes. He finished with a strawberry flan piled up with cream, and with coffee. He felt much better then, and his head was almost clear.

He went out, finding the fog less thick than he had noticed

it before; it was often clearer in the heart of the West End than on its perimeter. Traffic was moving slowly, and there was plenty of time for him to cross the road nearer Leicester Square. He did not hurry.

A car, crawling until then, roared and hurtled forward. On the instant he knew this was the awaited attack. He heard the first growling note of the engine, jerked his head towards the left, and flung himself forward. His left toe caught the kerb, he tripped, snatched his foot upwards, but could not stop himself from falling. The pavement was narrow. He turned his left shoulder towards a huge plate-glass window which loomed in front of him. He heard the deafening roar of the engine. He hit the glass. There was a great boom of sound, he felt the window give, and immediately afterwards there came a report like a rocket exploding. He slithered down the window. The car was a hundred feet behind him now, a dark shape and a misty red light. Someone was standing close by. He fell in a curiously crouching way, almost stunned by the force of the impact.

The man came further forward, and others came running. Dawlish was actually at full length, gasping for breath. He saw a man's feet just ahead of him, and thought the man was going to kick him. He covered his head with his arms, desperately, but the man stopped and said breathlessly:

'Are you all right?'

'Eh?' Dawlish muttered. He opened his eyes, and saw that the other was squatting down by his side. 'Eh?' Oh, yes, I'm all right.' He began to get up, feeling as if he were drunk. The man steadied him. 'Thanks,' he muttered. 'Car nearly got me. Did you see it?'

'Thought you were a goner,' the other said.

Then two men passed by.

By that time half a dozen others had gathered near and people were standing and staring from the other side of the road; but two men came walking along at a swinging pace. and actually went past. Dawlish noticed them because of the sharp rap-rap-rap of their footsteps on the pavement; neither fog nor a crowd was going to slow them down.

One of the men said: 'Oh, it was very funny, very funny indeed. He was afraid to sit down for weeks after that.'

And he chuckled.

There was no possible doubt that this was the voice of the telephone.

* * * * *

The man had been looking towards his companion and away from Dawlish. He wore a bowler hat, and it was impossible to see his face clearly; but it was the man of the telephone. Dawlish was standing upright then, very badly shaken, his head still ringing, his knees smarting where he had hit the ground, a dull ache in his left shoulder. He stared at the two men. They were passing beneath a lamp, and its misty, iridescent glow fell upon them, the second man, the man on the outside, had a mop of frizzy grey hair. Even more significant, he walked with the jaunty step and the swing of the shoulders by which Dawlish had been haunted all day.

'God!' he breathed. 'Let me——'

He thrust himself forward, past the man who had come to his aid. Three people, close to him, dodged hurriedly to one side. Dawlish missed a step. He was dizzy, he could hardly keep his feet, and the two men were almost invisible now, just shapes in the fog.

Dawlish roared, '*Police!*' and tried to go forward again, but knew that if he didn't stop he would fall. He stopped, swaying. A policeman was on the other side of the road, waiting for a car to pass. '*Get those two men!*' Dawlish cried, but the two men had disappeared in the fog already, and there were half a dozen different turnings they could take.

The laughter seemed to float back to him on the arms of the fog.

The policeman came up. . . .

But the police had not been able to prevent the attack, remember.

\* \* \* \* \*

'They knew I was at the restaurant,' Dawlish found himself thinking desperately. 'They had the car waiting. They passed within a yard of me.'

It was very cold.

He was sweating.

CHAPTER XIV

TIM

THE first thing Dawlish saw when he turned into the mews, very cautiously because it was difficult to see the kerb, was a faint diffusion of light from a window of the flat. He pulled up close to the wall. The fog picked up the glow of the car's lights and almost dazzled him. He saw where he was for fully half a minute. The truth was that he had not fully recovered from the shock of what had happened in St. Martin's Lane. The fact that his enemies had trailed him when the police had not was one of the most alarming things.

These men, who hated him so, were dedicated to his destruction. The police were simply doing their job.

A figure loomed out of the fog, and Dawlish felt his heart begin to pound. The man said:

'That you, Mr. Dawlish?'

'Yes,' Dawlish said. 'Hallo.' He opened the door and got out—and saw that it was impossible to see to the other side of the mews entrance; a man creeping by on rubber soles might actually pass them as they stood talking. 'Still on your own?'

'Three of us here now, sir, we're not going to take any more chances. One on the other side of the entrance, another by the steps leading to your place.'

'Good,' Dawlish said, fervently. 'What's that light?'

'Oh—that's Mr. Jeremy, sir. I checked with Mr. Trevitt that it was all right to let him pass.'

'Well, well!' Dawlish's spirits rose, bounding. 'How long has he been here?'

'About an hour, sir. No one could tell him where he could find you so he decided that the best thing was to wait.'

'Couldn't be better,' Dawlish said. 'Thanks again.' He stepped towards the dim light, which became slightly brighter as he neared it. The fog was so thick that even though he knew the mews well, and the light was there to guide him, he went cautiously over the slippery cobbles. Another man loomed up, and said:

'Who's that?'

'Dawlish.'

'Just a moment, sir, if you please.' A yellow torch light shone into Dawlish's face, and then dropped away. 'That's all right, Mr. Dawlish, but we have to be sure.'

'Yes,' said Dawlish. 'You're doing me a world of good.' He went up the steps, slid the key into the lock very cautiously, opened the door an inch and then opened his lips and gave a cry which was startlingly like the call of an owl. It echoed about the mews, and seemed to fill the flat. Almost at once there was thump of footsteps, a door was pulled open, and a tall, thin man came striding along, his face in

81

shadows. He switched on the hall light and the face became Tim Jeremy's, lean, lined, slashed with a vivid white grin.

'You old so-and-so!' he greeted, and their hands gripped. I didn't hear a sound before your call.' He put his head back, opened his mouth wide, and emitted the same sound as Dawlish; here, it was resoundingly loud. It also carried them back over the years, to dark nights and moonlit nights in occupied Europe, the call proving vital when they had been dropped from the same aircraft but landed perhaps a mile apart.

Tim's expression changed.

'Pat,' he said, 'just for half a minute I forgot what's happened.'

'I know,' Dawlish said, more soberly. 'I did, too.' They went into the large, low-ceilinged room where he had seen Ted Beresford that morning, and went on: 'It couldn't be worse.' . . .

'Felicity all right?'

'Trivett's looking after her.'

'Thanks be for mercies,' Tim said. 'I was afraid——' he broke off. 'I picked up a news item from a B.B.C. broadcast in Monte. Caught the first 'plane back from Nice.'

'Wonderful,' Dawlish said.

'Where's Ted?'

'Up at Oxford, doped I hope.'

'No need to ask how he's taken it,' Jeremy said. He took out cigarettes, proffered them, and lit up. 'Any beer in, do you know?'

'It you haven't looked, you're slipping,' Dawlish remarked. 'Yes, a few bottles.' He went with Jeremy into the kitchen. There were three bottles of beer in the refrigerator, several more standing in the larder. They took out two cold bottles, put two warm ones in the frig.

'What lessons we learn from America,' Jeremy said, and fumbled in a drawer for a bottle-opener.

Dawlish was watching him closely. It was nearly six months since they had met, and Jeremy looked berry brown and fit, his grey eyes had a gleam, He, Ted Beresford and Dawlish had known each other since their preparatory school days, and lived, fought and worked together since. A few years ago Jeremy had run into wife trouble. There had been a divorce, and not long afterwards it had looked as if he would marry again, but he had not; instead he was a bachelor with a roving eye and a cynical turn of mind; his thin face could look positively ugly, and yet there was a lean strength and attractiveness about it.

He poured out the beer.

'Let's have the whole story,' he said, and they went into the big room, each dropped into a large armchair. Each left the smaller one, with the low arms, in which Joan usually sat; Joan should have been sitting by the electric fire, sewing or knitting. Dawlish began to talk. That was a good thing in more ways than one, for it enabled him to go over everything that had happened, and he could see some of the things in better perspective. Jeremy smoked four cigarettes, but did not interrupt.

When Dawlish finished, he said: 'Not exactly a rest cure, Pat. What's your next move?'

Dawlish didn't answer, and Jeremy did not speak again. Over the years it had been a natural development that Dawlish should cogitate a problem, reason out the best course of action, and put it to the others. Usually they first tested it with argument and finally accepted it; occasionally they riddled it with ridicule. The one constant factor had been that Dawlish always had some proposition to make. Now he was silent for a long time, Jeremy took the two empty bottles out, went back for more, came and stood in the doorway, tall enough to touch the lintel with his head.

Dawlish said slowly, heavily: 'We've got to hit back, Tim. Soon. Hard.'

'Ah. How?' Tim advanced, a bottle in each hand and a slight head at the top of each. 'Given up thinking that it's worth working on Gorman?'

'I don't think we'll get anything out of him.'

'The floosie?'

Dawlish found his seriousness punctured by a grin.

'I don't think Eileen Parish would appreciate being called a floosie. I think she would help, if she could. Don't ask me if I'm sure, because I'm not. She might have expected me, and could be working with him. There is the other pair—Johnny Chalke and Fred Holsen. Trivett said——'

The telephone bell rang.

Dawlish felt his nerves jump at the first ting, and was sharply annoyed with himself. Jeremy simply glanced round; he hadn't been conditioned to telephone calls in this case. Dawlish stretched out a hand, lifted the receiver, and wondered if he would hear a man with a laughing voice, a man who was undoubtedly somewhere in London.

It was Trivett.

'Hallo, Pat,' Trivett said. 'So you know Tim's back.'

'Yes, and right on the ball,' Dawlish replied.

'I couldn't be more glad,' Trivett said. 'Two things I think you should know. I've heard from Oxford that Ted has been given a sedative. His sister-in-law seems to have a lot of influence on him, and he certainly won't be back in London until tomorrow midday.'

'Fine,' said Dawlish.

'The other thing is that one of our officers followed the two men who walked past you in St. Martin's Lane this evening,' Trivett announced, quite calmly. 'Another of them tried to follow the car, a black Ford Zephyr, but it got away in the fog. So did the men, when they knew they were being tailed, but not before our chap had a good look at them.'

Dawlish's heart was pounding again.

'Recognize them?'

'He recognized the smaller of the two, one who might just answer to your description of the tramp.'

'Ah,' said Dawlish. 'Who?'

'George Tenby,' Trivett answered. 'You probably won't know him by name, but he once went down for three years on a job which we always thought was done for Johnny Chalke. We never proved it, we can't be sure that Tenby and Chalke ever worked together, but that smudged fingerprint tallies with Tenby's, too,' Trivett paused.

'Bill,' breathed Dawlish, 'thanks.'

'Tenby's been out of jail for five years,' went on Trivett. 'He's an insurance agent for one or two of the smaller companies; he always did have a good spiel. He's in the telephone directory, too.'

'Fine,' Dawlish said. 'I'll look him up.'

'We could go and question him,' Trivett pointed out, 'but the fact is that we couldn't do anything more, and if we questioned him it probably wouldn't do much good, and might do harm by warning him we're on his trail. He was seen walking past you just after you'd nearly been run down, but there were a dozen witnesses to say that he didn't do anything else.'

'I know,' said Dawlish. 'Thanks, Bill.'

'Pat.'

'Yes.'

'No one wants to get to the bottom of this more than I do. No one knows better than I how you feel about it. But as a citizen, Tenby has certain rights—as many rights as you. If you abuse any of his rights, then the law is on his side. We are the law. It's no use telling you not to take any risks, but . . .'

Dawlish grinned.

'I know, Bill. It isn't what I do that matters, it's whether I'm found out. You couldn't tell me anything else about Tenby, could you? I mean, married, single, that kind of thing.'

'Married, no children, Pat . . .'

'Thanks,' Dawlish said. 'Thanks. I seem to have said that before. After all, if a man's married and someone makes threats against his wife, he's always inclined to soften up, isn't he?' He was already thumbing the telephone directory, while Jeremy stood glowering down at him. 'I'll be seeing you, Bill.' Dawlish banged down the receiver, glanced up at Jeremy, but didn't speak for what seemed a long time. At last, he felt that there was a chance of striking back, and Trivett had made it crystal clear that the police had to leave Tenby to him, at this stage. And he must not slip up.

'Well?' Tim was stung to ask.

'We've got a date,' Dawlish announced quietly. 'Get ready to use that telephone, will you?' Jeremy picked it up, as Dawlish ran his forefinger down the T columns, and stopped at an entry: 'Tenby, Geo. T. Insce., 28 Downs Road, St. John's Wood. Abbey 13245.' As he uttered the number, Jeremy began to dial. 'Thanks,' said Dawlish again, and he took the receiver away as the other finished dialling, then sat on the arm of the chair and listened to the ringing sound.

It was a little after nine-thirty.

There was a break in the ringing, and a woman answered in a pleasant voice, 'This is Claire Tenby.'

'Mr. Tenby in?' Dawlish demanded. His voice sounded as if he had been born within shouting distance of Bow Bells.

'I'm afraid he's not,' said Claire Tenby. 'Who——'

'Any idea when he'll be in?'

'It's difficult to say on a night like this,' the woman answered, 'but I wouldn't expect him to be later than eleven o'clock. Can I give him a message?'

'No thanks,' Dawlish replied. 'I'll call him in the morning. I got 'n insurance claim to make. Good night.' He put down the receiver, turned, and saw Jeremy coming in with their coats and hats. 'Yes,' Dawlish said to him, 'that's about the size of it, Tim. The problem is going to be getting to Downs

Road through the fog, but once we're there the fog's going to help.'

'What's on that thing you call a mind?' demanded Jeremy.

Dawlish said, heavily: 'Tim, we're in a spot. *I'm* in a spot, rather. What happened to Joan could happen to Fel, and Trivett is almost sure that it will happen to me. This Tenby has rights as a citizen, as Trivett reminded me, and so has his wife. I've got rights, too. I can't stop at trifles to make sure they're secure. I'm going to take Mrs. Tenby away from the bosom of her family, and then work on Tenby.'

'Ah,' said Jeremy, owlishly. 'Reprisals in kind. I wish I could see in the dark,' he added. 'It's just possible that the fog's lifting a bit.' He opened the door, and thick fog eddied in; they could hardly see the man on duty at the foot of the steps. 'Well, let's see how far it is to walk?'

'Too far,' Dawlish declared.

\* \* \* \* \*

The journey took them just under an hour. Here and there the fog thinned out a little but in St. John's Wood it seemed thicker than ever. Jeremy knew Downs Road, and there was a garage with all its lights on quite near the corner. Dawlish drove past, parked round the corner in Downs Road, then groped his way with Jeremy towards Number 28.

There was a light at the fanlight, showing the number mistily through the gloom.

## CHAPTER XV

## REPRISALS

THE house was one of a terrace, and as far as they could judge, there were only two stories. Two street-lamps spread a faint, diffused glow, but it was impossible to see across the road. In front of all the houses there was a little area, about five feet deep, protected by a small coping and—in the case of Number 28—a privet hedge. Dawlish and Jeremy stepped through the iron gate, closed it without making a sound, and studied the fanlight. They could just make out the outline of the windows, to their right.

'What's the next move?' Jeremy whispered.

'Let's see if we can get in through that window,' Dawlish said. They went forward together, but it was not possible to see the catch of the sashcord window, and a torch made the fog seem thicker. Dawlish took out the knife which had forced the door of Eileen Parish's house, opened the same blade, and slid it between the two frames. He felt the catch. He pushed, and it gave slightly. He pushed harder, and it clicked back so loudly that they stood listening for anything to suggest that the noise had been heard.

No sound came.

Dawlish closed the blade and opened another, a short, stubby screwdriver. He levered the bottom window up an inch; after that it was easy to get his fingers underneath and open it wide.

'I'll get inside,' he said. 'You ring the front-door bell, I'll deal with whoever opens the door.'

'Right.'

Dawlish put one leg through the window, groped with his foot, found that the floor was carpeted, and stepped right inside. He stood shining his torch, confident that there was practically no risk of being seen. He saw the door, side-stepped a table and two chairs, and reached it. He opened it a crack. There was no wind outside, and no draught there. The light from the hall shone brightly in a long narrow sliver against the wall. He wondered how long Tim would be, then heard a bell ring. There was no other sound. He kept very still, and it seemed a long time before a door opened and footsteps tap-tapped in the passage. He manoeuvred so that he could see the passage, and a woman came within his line of vision. He could not really tell whether she was good looking, but she certainly had a figure, although she was on the plump side. She walked slowly, apparently not quite sure what to do, and Dawlish had an impression that she was nervous. She passed him. At the door she hesitated, but soon he heard the sound of a bolt being drawn. He stepped forward a little, so that he could see her stretching up to the top bolt. A moment later she slid a chain along its channel and opened the door a few inches.

'Who is it?' she demanded.

'Sorry to worry you,' Jeremy said, and he sounded really apologetic, 'but I wonder if you know where a Mrs. Jensen lives.'

'*Who?*'

'Mrs. Jensen.'

'No. I've never heard of the name,' this woman said hurriedly. 'My name is Tenby. I'm sorry.' She began to close the door, and Dawlish heard her quick breathing, and no longer doubted that she was scared of being on her own. He stood behind her as she stretched forward to thrust the door to. She wore a black skirt which fitted skin tight, and a thick yellow cardigan. She had a nice shape, plump legs and exceptionally small ankles. Before she could find out that the door wouldn't close, Dawlish took a step forward, slid his right hand round her face and pressed her tightly back against him.

She jumped wildly, and something of her scream escaped through Dawlish's fingers.

'All right,' Dawlish said, sharply. 'Keep still, and I won't hurt you. Keep still.'

She went still. He felt her shaking; there was no doubt of her terror. He maintained the pressure of his hand and slid his left arm round her, pressing against her plump little belly. 'Turn round slowly,' he said, 'and remember I won't hurt you provided you don't make a fuss.' He helped her to turn round, and went on: 'Now, go back towards the room you came from.

It was a living-room with a television set in one corner, its screen blank, a comfortable three-piece suite about the fireplace, a dining-table against the window, four dining-chairs; there was a touch of quality about everything, including the green-and-biege curtains, the pale green wallpaper, the brick-built fireplace, the red mohair upholstery. A door led out of this room, presumably into the kitchen, but the door was closed. The curtains were of heavy velvet or velour.

Dawlish took his hands away as Tim came in.

The woman spun round, her face distorted with terror, and kicked at his shins. The pointed toe of her right shoe caught him just above the ankle, making him wince, but she missed with another kick, and lost her balance. Dawlish snatched at her tiny hands, and wrapped both wrists in his great left hand.

'Stop it or you'll get hurt,' he said roughly.

She opened her mouth to scream, so he prodded her in the stomach with his fingers. She gasped, gulped, and made a sound like air escaping from a balloon with a slow puncture.

'I tell you I won't hurt you if you keep quiet,' he said again, 'but if you make any more fuss you'll get hurt all right.'

He held her hands tightly, and looked into her blazing

88

eyes. He realized with a sickening sense of shame that she must be feeling much as Joan had; as Felicity would, in like circumstances. She was gasping for breath. Her plump little body was too tightly confined, she bulged a little from a lower-than-average neckline. As she stared at him, he heard a movement from behind and then she looked over her shoulder and obviously saw Tim.

'No!' she gasped, but it wasn't a scream, it wasn't a sound likely to carry outside this room, it was nearly a whisper. 'No, don't hurt me, please. There's nothing here worth taking, I haven't any jewellery, *hardly* any jewellery. I've an old fur coat, you can take that, you——'

She broke off.

'Just answer a few questions,' Dawlish ordered, 'and keep your voice low. Does your husband still work for Johnny Chalke?'

She gasped; and even if she denied it, even if she screamed a denial, he felt quite sure that she knew that Tenby did work for Chalke.

'No!' she gasped at last. 'No, he used to, but Chalke let him down once. He went to prison for it, he hasn't worked for Chalke since he came out. That's God's truth!'

'Where was your husband this morning!'

'He—he was out. He's always out during the day, he has to earn a living, hasn't he? You can't expect him to be hanging about the house all day.'

'What car does he run?'

'He——'

'*What car?*'

'He—he runs a Ford, a black Zephyr, he's had it for years. He has to have a decent car, he's got to earn a good living, putting up a front's half the battle with an insurance man. You can't blame him for running a good car!'

'Is it black?'

'Ye—yes. Yes, it is, but there are thousands of black Zephyrs, what difference does it make?'

'Where was he last night?'

'I don't know——' she began, and then she closed her eyes for a moment, screwing them up as Beresford had that morning, and when she spoke again it was in a lower-pitched voice, from a kind of fear very different from the terror she had first felt. Then, she had been in fear of death. 'He—he was in all the evening! He—he's usually in during the evening, it's most unusual for him to be out, but he had a special client he had to see tonight. I tell you he had to see a special client!'

'What's the client's name?'

'*I don't know*! How do you expect me to know all his customers? I don't work with him, I'm only his wife. I won't answer any more questions, I've got a right——'

Tim Jeremy said, 'She's lying right and left.'

'I'm not!' she screamed. 'I——' she saw Dawlish move his hand towards her, to silence her. She stopped on the instant, and went on in a whisper! 'I won't make any noise, and—and I'm not lying.'

'Where was Tenby last night?'

She gulped. 'He—he had to go out on a special job, it was —it was out of London somewhere. I don't know where he went. He—he's running straight, I tell you, he's paid for what he did years ago.'

'Does he do Chalke's insurance?'

The woman said, helplessly, despairingly: 'I suppose so. Chalke owes him something, doesn't he? I suppose he does. But what are you going to do with me? Who are you? What are you asking all these questions for?'

Dawlish said, 'You're coming with us for a day or two, Claire.'

'*No*!'

'Don't make a fuss, and you'll be perfectly all right.'

'I won't come with you, I won't! You've got no right to——'

'Claire,' Dawlish interrupted, 'if Tenby's in the clear, there's no need for either of you to worry. If he's not, he can worry but you don't have to. My car's outside. You've got three minutes to put some clothes on and come with me. If you shout or try to run away, you'll be making a big mistake.'

She didn't answer, but turned to go upstairs with Jeremy and, two minutes later, came down wearing a mink coat. It looked comparatively new, too, and Dawlish put its value at over a thousand pounds. She wore a mink hat, rather like a beret, and under it her blue eyes seemed very bright and her red cheeks glowed. He felt sure that directly they reached the street, probably as soon as they opened the front door, she would start screaming.

'Claire,' Dawlish said softly, and she turned round towards him. Jeremy, just behind her, knew exactly what to do. He struck her on the nape of the neck with the side of his hand, and she collapsed without knowing what had hit her.

Dawlish held her upright.

'Can't say that's my favourite occupation,' Jeremy said. 'I'll carry her. Any need for a gag?'

''Fraid so,' Dawlish said. 'You needn't be rough. Park her in the back of the car, and come straight back. Better keep an eye open in case Tenby arrives,' Dawlish went on. He leaned the woman towards Jeremy, and was tight-lipped as he opened the door. The fog shrouded everything and everybody; there could not have been a better night than this.

\* \* \* \* \*

Dawlish found nothing of interest in the dining-room or the front room, except the fact that furniture, ornaments and furnishings were of good quality. Upstairs there were four rooms, one of them an office, and on the desk was a brief-case, with a dossier on Gorman by it. He felt a quickening of excitement as he began to look through the records of Tenby's business. Tenby represented three small insurance companies, and his turnover was in the region of fifty thousand pounds a year, on a 2½ per cent commission an annual income of about twelve hundred pounds. The kind of mink coat that his wife had would cost years of scrimping and saving. Then he found out that Johnny Chalke was insured for nearly fifty thousand pounds in endowment policies. Chalke also had insurance cover for twenty-odd houses in different parts of London, and for several shops. Dawlish wondered if the police knew how much property the ex-convict owned.

There was a personal bank-account statement; Claire Tenby had two hundred and twenty-one pounds, and a hundred and ten pounds in National Savings Certificates.

Dawlish kept searching, and came upon an endowment policy for ten thousand pounds in Maurice Gorman's name, taken out nine years ago; there were still six years of premiums to pay. The records showed that payments had been maintained while Gorman was in prison.

Holsen wasn't mentioned anywhere, but Eileen Parish was insured for just over a thousand pounds, the premium payable yearly.

That was all Dawlish found.

He went into the main bedroom. The furniture was ex-quisite—twin beds, with pale-blue satin-quilted head-boards, the most expensive carpet and curtains and décor. He searched until he found a locked jewel box in a recess in the wardrobe, and also found the key in the dressing-table. In the box were at least four thousand pounds' worth of jewels.

He felt still easier in his mind, for Claire Tenby must know that her husband did not buy her this kind of present from an insurance agency income.

Dawlish went downstairs again and was turning to step into the dining-room to see if he could find himself a drink, when he remembered the door underneath the stairs. He opened it, saw some outdoor clothes hanging behind the door, and more on hooks opposite him. To the right there was a flight of steps leading down to a cellar.

He was about to go down when he heard a sound at the front door, and a moment later the old familiar warning, the low-pitched cry of an owl, came clearly through the letter-box.

The shutter of the box clicked.

Dawlish stepped swiftly into the dining-room. then reached the door as the key sounded in the lock. A moment later the front door closed, and a man called:

'I'm back, honey!'

The man came walking briskly towards the open dining-room door.

CHAPTER XVI

TENBY'S FINGERPRINTS

'You there, sweet?' Tenby called.

He was just outside the room, and Dawlish heard a rustling movement which suggested that he was taking off his coat. A door opened, and obviously the man was putting hat and coat inside a cupboard under the stairs. So far there was no kind of alarm in his voice, and he spoke much as any man coming home after a heavy day's work.

'My, I could do with a Scotch-and-soda!'

He stepped into the dining-room and the light shone on his frizzy hair and his spare, square shoulders; he was the tramp, beyond any doubt. Dawlish glanced down at his shoes; they were highly polished, but black. He was exceptionally well-dressed, and it was the jauntiness and the shape of his head and the back of his neck, as well as his hair, which made identification so certain.

'Claire!' he called, more sharply, and turned round. But he turned with his back to Dawlish, and started towards the passage again. 'Are you upstairs?'

Dawlish said, 'How do you know she isn't where Joan Beresford is?'

Tenby spun round both arms raised in an attitude of abject surrender. He was utterly astounded, mouth wide open, eyes rounded in terror. Dawlish hit him once in the stomach. Tenby gave a queer little gasping sound, and staggered backwards. His right hand made a circular movement, as if he were trying to get at something. Dawlish took his left wrist, hauled him forward, twisted him round, and dipped a hand into the right-hand coat pocket. He felt the cold steel of an automatic. He drew it out cautiously, and slipped it into his own pocket, touching only the barrel; any prints on the butt would remain. He let Tenby go, and gave him a push; he came up against the dining-table, heavily and painfully, making a moaning sound.

Dawlish stood contemplating him.

Here was the man who had put that nitro-glycerine in the doorway of Four Ways and beneath the Allard, presumably who had put it in the sugar, too. Here was a killer as deadly as killers came, and yet found it something to be gay and jaunty about. Here was a man who did not rate for a moment's pity and and—here was the man who had probably strangled Joan.

Tenby clutched the back of a chair, tried to straighten up, pulled the chair from beneath the table, and collapsed on to it. Dawlish still watched in stony silence. He twisted round, looking into Dawlish's face. He had lost all his colour, and his newly shaven face was sweating. His brows were drawn together, as if with pain, and he was breathing through his mouth.

'Well,' Dawlish said, 'how do you know your wife hasn't gone the way Joan Beresford went?'

Tenby made no attempt to answer.

Dawlish went on: 'That's where you're going, Tenby, unless you answer all my questions.'

The man tried to speak but couldn't get words out. It was not wholly because he was in pain, and breathless. He was like a man in the ring who had been put down, and was taking full advantage of the count; he would probably get up at eight or nine. He shifted his position a little, facing Dawlish more squarely.

Dawlish said, 'Do you smoke?'

'Ye-yes,' Tenby muttered.

'Hand me your cigarette-case,' Dawlish ordered, and the man obeyed, as if he could not understand what this was about. The cigarette-case was of polished silver, exactly what Dawlish wanted. Dawlish took it, and placed in on a corner of the table, then took out the glossy print of the blown-up photograph which had been found on the insulation tape outside Ted Beresford's flat. He took out a small magnifying glass and, glancing at Tenby from time to time, studied the print on the cigarette case and compared it with the one which Trivett had given him.

One print was identical. He knew enough about the system to be sure that this was a tented arch which would never be duplicated; and there was a tiny scar, rather like the shape of a fish's tail, in the centre of it. He placed the cigarette-case and the print into his inside coat pocket, tucked the magnifying glass away, and saw that Tenby's eyes were narrowed and there was a glint in them. Cunning? He was going to hit back at any moment, Dawlish suspected. Had he another weapon, or would he try to fight?

'So you killed her,' Dawlish said flatly.

'I didn't kill anyone.'

'You killed her,' Dawlish accused, 'and you had a partner. Who was it?'

'You're wrong, Dawlish! I didn't kill——'

'You shouldn't have left your prints in the car, and you shouldn't have left them on Mrs. Beresford's ear-rings,' Dawlish said.

This impression that Tenby was going to fight back faded; he seemed to collapse, and turned a sickly grey, as if he believed that the evidence against him was deadly.

'Who was with you?' Dawlish demanded.

Tenby didn't answer.

'Tenby, there are some things you have to know,' Dawlish said, in a stony voice. 'If the police ever get you alive, you'll have a fair trial. The police are funny that way. If I have to deal with you myself, you won't get a trial at all. You murdered the wife of my closest friend. You came within an ace of murdering my own wife. You nearly murdered me. Don't get any idea that I'm going to play by the rules. In this affair I make my own. I've taken your wife away. She seems an inoffensive little woman, and she's probably fond of you. She may not know that you're a murderer, but she does know that you're a thief, and that her coat and her jewels are stolen property. So she isn't just an innocent victim. She's in deadly danger. I mean to find out everyone who's involved in this campaign against me, and I don't care what I have to do to get the information. If your wife dies you might close up, but the fact that she's dead will open other mouths. Don't make any mistakes, and don't fool yourself into thinking that I won't do it. Got that?'

Tenby muttered: 'Yes! Yes, Dawlish, but my wife doesn't know anything, she——'

'Beresford's wife didn't either.'

'Dawlish, I——' Tenby began, but he could not finish; it seemed as if he suddenly realized the uselessness of words. He was frightened for his life, and that was how it should be. He might possibly know enough to enable Dawlish to end this nightmare within a few hours.

'I couldn't help myself,' he muttered, hoarsely. 'I'm—I'm not a killer, Dawlish. I—I didn't mean to kill. I didn't think it was going to come to murder.

'But you strangled Mrs. Beresford.'

'It—it was only to make her unconscious!' Tenby asserted desperately. 'I didn't think she would die, it—it was an accident!'

'It won't be an accident if your wife dies,' retorted Dawlish. 'It will be with malice aforethought, and she will know the same kind of terror that Beresford's wife suffered.' Every word seemed clipped, every word conveyed something of his hatred. He could have moved forward and squeezed this man's life out of him, he hated him so much. 'Who was with you?'

'I—I can't tell you!'

'Who was with you?'

'If I squeal, I'll be killed!'

'And if you don't, both you and your wife will be,' Dawlish retorted. 'Who was with you?'

'Oh, God,' Tenby gasped, and he wiped his right hand across his forehead; a trembling hand. 'Dawlish, do what you like to me, but my wife——'

'You made the rules.'

'Dawlish! I——' Tenby took in a deep breath, and said in a quavering voice: 'If—if I tell you who was with me, will you let my wife go?'

'I'll want some extra information,' Dawlish said. 'Don't keep wasting time. Who was with you last night?'

Tenby didn't answer at once. His body seemed to tremble, and his hands were shaking as he put them to his forehead. But Dawlish saw that he had shifted his position, that his feet were firmly on the floor by the side of the table. Dawlish went forward casually, as if he had not noticed this: and Tenby sprang at him.

In his hand was a flick-knife, the light glinting on the blade.

Dawlish simply put out his left leg, and Tenby rammed himself against it. The air was driven out of his body with a gusty, anguished groan, he staggered two tottering paces backwards and then doubled up; the knife fell from his hand and stuck, quivering in the floor. Dawlish bent down and picked it up, then looked at it thoughtfully. It was of foreign manufacture, a beautiful piece of steel, its point as sharp as a dagger.

It would be several minutes before Tenby came round well enough to talk, and Dawlish left him, holding his breath in agony, and went to the front door. He opened it, and saw Tim in the porch.

'All right?'

'He's one of the men we're after,' Dawlish said. 'I don't think I'll be long. We might have to take him with us.'

'Thought of where?'

'Yes.'

'Where?'

'Chalke's place, in Pimlico.'

'Might be an idea,' agreed Jeremy, 'I'll do some thinking, too. Claire's sleeping the sleep of the unjust. The fog's clearing a bit, there's a wind which keeps shifting it in patches.'

'It'll do all we want of it,' Dawlish said. 'Anyone about?'

'Only two people passed since I've been out here.'

'I won't be long,' Dawlish said, and went back into the passage. When he reached the dining-room Tenby was drawing in noisy, shuddering breaths, and there was no pretence about the trembling. Dawlish sat back in a large armchair, lit a cigarette and watched him. The frizzy grey hair caught the light from the lamp and from the fire. The pallor of his cheeks was almost unbelievable, and his lips were sickly grey. He dragged himself to a crouching position, dropped on to the chair and leaned forward, his head between his knees. Dawlish got up, went into the kitchen, filled a jug with

96

# Around £13,000 can make your retirement as carefree as this.

It's very easy to make sure of a happy and secure retirement. You just take out a Prudential Endowment Assurance.

For example, if you're a man aged 30 next birthday, a monthly premium of £12.50 would give you a guaranteed minimum sum of £5,000 at age 65. But this sum would be increased by bonuses, and a £5,000 policy for a similar term maturing on April 1st, 1974, would have given you a lump sum of £12,970.* Of course, bonuses can go down as well as up. But in the past the trend has always been a steady rise.

For the full story of how to make your retirement secure and happy, just fill in the coupon and send us the card. It won't cost you anything to find out.

And it could give you peace of mind. At the very least.

## Prudential

Purely by way of interest, I'd like full details of your Endowment Assurance policies.

Name

Address

Prudential Assurance Company Limited

*Applies to U.K. only.

BUSINESS REPLY SERVICE
LICENCE NO. KE 1511

The Chief General Manager
The Prudential Assurance Co Ltd
142 Holborn Bars
London EC1N 2NH

water from the cold tap, came back and tipped the lot over Tenby's head. Tenby gave a convulsive shiver, and threw his head back. Water coursed down his cheeks from hair which had suddenly become flat and lifeless; it soaked his collar and tie, and dropped on to the carpet.

'Who was with you last night?' Dawlish asked, without any change of tone.

'It was—it was someone you don't know,' Tenby answered. 'A—a man named Pope, Jackie Pope. He——'

'Does Pope work for Chalke?'

'Chalke—Chalke's got nothing to do with it!'

'Think again, Tenby,' Dawlish said.

'Chalke's been a good friend of mine since I came out of jug, but he's got nothing to do with this,' Tenby declared hoarsely. 'It was Pope who put the proposition to me, and—and I hate your guts anyway, Dawlish! You put a brother of mine away once, he's still up at Strangeways. But we didn't mean to kill Mrs. Beresford, we——'

'What did you propose to do with the nitro? Make Chineses crackers with it? Why don't you grow up, Tenby? If you don't tell me who paid you and who is behind this, you'll really get hurt, and——'

'It isn't Chalke!' gasped Tenby. 'It's Gorman!'

He named Maurice Gorman as if he were afraid of the consequences of doing so; and he had not seemed so frightened before. He sat doubled up, head raised so as to stare into Dawlish's face, and when Dawlish gave no answer, he went on hurriedly:

'Gorman wanted Chalke to have a go at you, but Chalke's got too much at stake, he wasn't going to take any chances. When he came out of the Moor he told me what Gorman had been after, he just wouldn't touch the job. Gorman tried everyone you've ever helped to put inside, he——'

'You're forgetting something,' Dawlish interrupted, coldly.

'Dawlish, I swear to you——'

'You're forgetting that Gorman hasn't enough money to pay you the kind of rates you'd want for a job like this.'

Tenby gaped, and actually straightened up.

'Gorman hasn't got——' He broke off, gasped and then gave a queer kind of wheezing laugh. Laughing hurt him, and he pressed his hands against his stomach, as if to try to stop himself. When a paroxysm of mingled laughter and coughing had subsided, he said in a tinny voice: 'He made you fall for that, did he? You're not so clever as I thought you were.'

He began to laugh and cough again.

## CHAPTER XVII

## UNKNOWN RICHES?

DAWLISH stared at the man as he sat there, hand pressed against his stomach as if to ease the agony of laughter, and yet not able to stop himself. Of course, he was suffering from shock and fear, that was partly the cause of the uncontrollable laughter, but—he also thought this situation funny.

Would it seem funny to him, in these circumstances, unless there was a real edge to it?

Dawlish felt his hands clenching and unclenching; hating this man and yet facing the fact that Tenby was not in this alone. He might be telling the simple truth; that could be checked. The other man, Jackie Pope, couldn't be far away. He, Dawlish, might feel like breaking Tenby's neck, but he had come here to find out not only who had murdered Joan, but to make sure that there could be no danger to Felicity or himself.

He hadn't done that yet.

As Tenby's paroxysm subsided, Dawlish went into the kitchen again, and came back with a glass of water. Tenby was leaning back in his chair and wheezing. He grabbed the glass, tipped it back, drank as if he were dying of thirst, and gasped as he put the glass down.

'Th—th—thanks.'

'There are two ways you can be dealt with,' Dawlish said. 'I can hand you over to the police when I'm ready, as I've told you, and they're nice and humane. Or I can deal with you myself. I am not in a humane mood. What's this about Gorman having a lot of money?'

'You—you and the Yard—never did find out the truth about Gorman,' answered Tenby. He spoke now as if he had a severe cold and had to force the words out, but there was a curious gloating expression in his face. 'You *thought* you knew it all. That's the trouble with you clever bastards, you think you know everything. Gorman's got more intelligence in his backside than you——'

'You can cut out the flowers.'

'Don't you like plain English?' sneered Tenby. 'Well, take it from me, Ma Vaze wasn't the first or the second or the third of Gorman's old dames. He had them by the dozen. He used different names every time, and when he didn't get the dough given to him, they left it to him in their wills. Up and down the country, I'd say that Gorman must have picked up a hundred thousand quid from credulous old women with more money than sense. Didn't you realize that, Dawlish? Didn't you know he was a proper ladies' man? There isn't a woman in the world who could stand out against Gorman if he really exerted himself. He's got charm, that's what he's got—charm. He hypnotizes them. Young or old, they all fall for him. And he's got the boodle stacked away all over the place, in different names. You thought you'd fixed Gorman when you sent him away, but you hadn't really started. What's more, he went inside meaning to get you just as soon as he came out. He'll do it, too. You might be able to break my neck, you can stop me, you can even kill Claire, but whatever you do to me won't stop Gorman. He's been planning this for seven years and he's got one of the cleverest minds in the country. How do you like *that*, Dawlish?'

Dawlish said flatly, 'Prove any part of this story.'

'All right,' breathed Tenby. 'I'll prove it here and now. Gorman's got fifty endowment policies for a thousand pounds each, taken out with different companies. I know, I fixed the deals for him, I've got the policies here. He used to take out ten-year policies and pay the premiums in a lump sum. He reckoned it was the safest way. In all my old books you'll find a record of the transactions, too. I've got the books in the cellar, if you don't believe me. Some of those endowments matured when he was in jail. He wrote and asked for the payments to be held up until he gave the word. He can put his hand on twenty thousand any time he wants to, and at a week or two's notice he can get double it, maybe treble it.' Tenby drew a deep breath, finished the water and then asked in a sneering voice: 'Think I'd work for nothing? You must be a bloody fool. Think Jackie Pope and me would take on a job like this for chicken feed? Know how we're getting paid? Gorman's assigned some of his endowments to us. It's easy to fix it that way, no one asks questions, a man can do what he likes with his own policies—a lot of men borrow on them. Well, Gorman's paying us this way. If you doubt it, get some pals of yours to find out from the insurance companies. We get our dough in six months' time.'

Tenby stopped, still breathing sibilantly.

It sounded more true than ever, but there was a needle of doubt in Dawlish's mind; why was the man talking so freely? Had he realized that he hadn't a chance of escape otherwise? Did he believe that if Dawlish was able to get Gorman, he would not worry about the less important men?

That was possible.

The vital thing was to check everything he said, and get the facts right.

Tenby said: 'You can go through my records and find out, Dawlish. I can even tell you the different names Gorman uses. He's Bertram C. Field, he's Charles F. Cotton, he's Martin Benn, he's . . .'

Two or three of the names struck a cord in Dawlish's mind; he had seen them in the books in the little office upstairs. He wanted to find a quick way of proving that Tenby was telling the truth, and after a tense pause, he asked:

'Who holds the policies?'

'*I* do.'

'Where?'

'In the safe in the cellar.'

Dawlish thought, 'I didn't go down there,' but that passed quickly. He thought, 'He could still be fooling me,' and wondered whether Tenby's emphasis on the cellar was really a way of making sure that he, Dawlish, went into it. Tenby was sitting and staring at him with narrowed eyes, and it was impossible to be sure that there was any cunning in them now.

Dawlish said, 'Come with me, Tenby,' waited for the man to get up, and pushed him ahead of him to the front door. 'Open the door,' he ordered, and Tenby threw a scared glance over his shoulder before obeying. A shadowy figure appeared out of the fog, which Dawlish thought was thinning.

'Tim?'

'Yes.'

'Is the car locked?'

'And the lady in it.'

'Come in for ten minutes, will you?' asked Dawlish, and pushed Tenby aside. Tenby stared at Jeremy as if more frightened of him than of Dawlish, and when the door had closed he said shrilly:

'Where's my wife? Where is she? What have you done to her?'

'She's having a nice sleep,' answered Jeremy, mildly, 'and she might even wake up again if her husband does what he's

100

told. Want a little psychological pressure on him, Pat?'

'Probably. He seems very anxious for me to go down in the cellar, and I thought we'd better make sure that there isn't a booby-trap. We'll send him down first.' Dawlish looked at Jeremy most of the time but suddenly switched his glance to Tenby; from the change in the man's expression he felt quite sure that the cellar had some kind of significance. But he did not show that he had noticed anything as he took Tenby's arm and said, 'Lead the way.'

Tenby turned, gulped, and went to the cupboard where he had hung his hat and coat; he switched on a light, which showed the cellar steps leading away from the little cloakroom. The steps were of stone, and he had to lower his head to avoid bumping it. Dawlish followed close behind him, watching for the slightest indication of the secret of the cellar. There wasn't a booby trap in the physical sense; there would not be a sudden explosion, or Tenby would be absolutely terrified. What else would it be? What could give Tenby hope?

As they reached the bottom step Dawlish thought:

'He'd feel better if he could get some help.'

There were two doors at the foot of the steps, one leading straight on, and the smell of coal came from it, while the light shone faintly on kindling woods and logs. The door on the left was closed, and when Tenby opened it and switched on another light, the walls showed up clean and white, and two of the walls were lined with steel shelving, on which documents were stacked; this was simply a storeroom for insurance papers. There were several steel filing cabinets, as well as a big old-fashioned safe in a corner. Dawlish looked about him carefully, and saw only one thing which seemed out of place.

Near the safe, on the wall, was a bell-push.

He saw Tenby glance at this.

He said: 'Get that safe unlocked, and let me see these different policies. I want to compare the handwriting.' Tenby took out a heavy ring of keys, and went straight to the safe, while Jeremy stood in the doorway, obviously puzzled. 'Tim,' Dawlish went on, 'unless Tenby is lying to us, Gorman managed to salt away a fortune, and he put it into endowment policies.'

'Well, well,' said Jeremy, blankly.

'And he took them out under different names, with Tenby aiding and abetting,' Dawlish went on. He watched Tenby pull open the heavy door of the safe, and saw the man move back as he did so. For a moment, Tenby was behind the safe door, close to the bell-push. Dawlish did not actually see him stretch out an arm and press it, but he noticed the movement of the man's head towards the wall, the kind of movement which he would make if he were leaning forward. Then Tenby came from behind the safe door, looking downwards, as if to hide the expression in his eyes. Dawlish stood back as the man began to search the shelves of the safe for documents. Dawlish beckoned Jeremy, who came forward with three long, soundless steps.

'He's called for help,' Dawlish whispered. 'Stay just inside this room, someone might come down the stairs.'

Jeremy nodded.

Tenby must have heard the whispering, for he glanced round, holding some papers in his right hand. He stared at Dawlish, who looked quite blank, and then came forward, thrusting the documents towards Dawlish.

'Here are five different policies,' he said huskily. 'All Gorman's, under different names. You ought to be able to see that the handwriting's the same on the signatures.'

Dawlish took the documents.

Near the safe was a small table, immediately beneath the light. Dawlish spread the large policies on their stiff, crinkly paper out on the desk, so that all the signatures were in line, alongside one another. There were some doubts about Bertram C. Field and Martin C. Benn; but there was no reasonable doubt that the signature for Bertram C. Field was in the same handwriting as Martin C. Benn; the capital B's and C's were identical. So were other capital and small letters in other signatures; in nearly every case the same rather broad-nibbed pen had been used; in most, the same purple ink.

'Satisfied?' demanded Tenby, and the question was almost a sneer. His manner had changed in the last few minutes, there was brightness in his eyes, and his worst fear had gone; he was quite sure that help would come. But there was no sound; nothing to suggest that anyone was coming down the stairs. Dawlish looked about the cellar. If help were coming, what would be the most likely way? Front door to front door? That would take some time, it would mean that whoever came would have to have a key, and there would always be the risk that the door would be bolted; the same was true of the back door, and of the windows. Which way then?

Cellars had party walls; the wall on his right was a party

102

wall to the house on the other side. There were sections of steel shelving along it, some of them full, some of them almost empty, and he saw that each section was about four feet wide. There was a slight gap at the place where the sections met, too.

He said clearly, 'Let's get upstairs, Tim,' and took Tenby's arm—and then clapped his right hand over Tenby's mouth, choking back any cry. Jeremy asked a silent question. Dawlish nodded vigorously towards the wall, and dropped his right hand to his pocket. He and Jeremy stepped swiftly towards the wall, and as he reached it, one of the sections of the steel shelving began to open.

Jeremy stood close to the shelves, on one side. Dawlish lifted Tenby bodily and carried him to a spot where they could not be seen by the man who was pushing the shelving back.

This man appeared, holding a gun in his right hand Dawlish could not see him properly, caught just a glimpse of his profile. As he came further in, Jeremy simply swung his right leg upwards, the toe of his shoe caught the man's wrist and sent the gun flying. Before he recovered from the shock, Jeremy had him by the wrist and dragged him into the cellar.

Dawlish said, in a mocking laughing voice, 'Jackie Pope, I presume?'

For this was the man who had been with Tenby in St. Martin's Lane; the man who found the whole affair so very funny.

CHAPTER XVIII

POPE

POPE reeled away from Jeremy as Jeremy let him go, gaping at Dawlish and Tenby. Dawlish released Tenby at the same time. Jeremy went to the steel shelving and pulled open the section which Pope had used. He stood framed against the opening for a moment, and then said:

'Not a sign of anyone else.'

'Push something in front of that shelving to make sure no one can pay us a surprise visit,' Dawlish said. He looked at Tenby, and was grinning; but there was no humour in his voice as he went on, 'You can be out-thought as easily as an ape,' he said. 'Supposing you start waking up to the fact that I can kill you, your wife and your friend Pope, and that no

103

one would ever be able to blame me for it? A couple of these nitro sachets of yours, for instance, and a shot from the door. Your wife's still in the car outside, and I couldn't let her live because she would recognize me.'

'Oh God!' Tenby groaned.

'And supposing you wake up to the fact that you won't get any help, even by praying,' Dawlish said. 'Pope! Who paid you to start this campaign against me and Beresford?'

Pope was a heavier-built man than Tenby, and looked ten years older. He wore a well-cut, dark-brown suit, and had a close-trimmed moustache. He hadn't yet recovered from the stupefying effect of the shock, but there was a strange look about him—the look of a clown. It was easy to believe that he would find laughter coming easily although now his big, rounded, brown eyes were aglow with fear.

'I—I don't know what you're talking about,' he managed to say. 'I don't know a thing about——'

'Pope,' Dawlish interrupted softly, 'this isn't a funny story any longer. Who told——'

'I——' began Tenby, and Dawlish whirled round to him savagely.

'*Keep your mouth shut!*'

Tenby backed away, biting his bottom lip as if trying desperately to make sure that his mouth didn't open. Pope's expression was even more scared. Dawlish strode towards him and he backed hurriedly away, but Jeremy was just behind him. With a casual movement he leaned forward, took Pope's right arm and thrust it upwards behind him in a hammerlock.

'Pope, who paid you?' Dawlish demanded.

Pope shot a terrified look at Tenby, as if asking, 'How much have you told him?' but Tenby kept biting his lips.

'Pope,' said Dawlish, very softly, 'you're full of a rollicking sense of humour, aren't you? You make telephone calls and utter foul threats and laugh like hell because it's so funny. Well see if this is anything to laugh about.' He shot out his hands, gripped Pope round his plump waist, and began to knead the man's flesh with his powerful fingers, as if he were tickling; but the strength of his fingers was so great, and he poked and prodded and kneaded so savagely, that Pope began to squirm and wriggle and try to tear himself free; but Jeremy had him tightly and helplessly. Pope began to gasp, then began to cough and try to protest and it was like an idiot's laughter.

'St—st—stop!' he tried to gasp. 'Do'—do'—don't!' The breath seemed to be jerked out of his body and the strength in Dawlish's fingers seemed to become greater, until Pope lost all his colour, sweat stood out on his forehead and upper lip and began to drip down, it looked as if in a moment he would faint.

Dawlish stopped.

Without any cue from Dawlish Jeremy let the man go. He staggered blindly and helplessly against the wall, and leaned against it, half-crouching, still gasping for breath, while Tenby stood on the other side of the cellar and gaped as if horror-stricken.

After a while, Dawlish said, 'Who paid you to kill Mrs. Beresford and to come after me?'

'Don't—don't touch me again,' Pope muttered, fearfully. 'Don't touch me! It was Gorman, Maurice Gorman, he fixed it with Tenby and me.'

* * * * *

After he had answered Dawlish, Pope crawled along the side of the cellar until he reached the table, then he sat on it; he looked as if his legs would not support him. Tenby was saying: 'I told you who it was, why don't you believe me? I told you who it was.' Both men were terrified; and neither had any idea what was likely to happen next. Dawlish didn't speak for what seemed a long time, and Jeremy, always content to act as a foil, stood negligently by the door, tall, lean, menacing.

Dawlish said at last, 'Believe them, Tim?'

'Could be true,' Jeremy conceded. 'They found it hard to say, didn't they? Just about what you'd expect from strangers to the truth. We could check.'

'How?'

'Pat, they killed Joan, remember,' Jeremy said, in a deceptively casual voice. 'They nearly blew you and Felicity into small pieces. Hanging is too good for them. A spot of beating up now would be rough justice, and would certainly loosen their tongues.' He looked round the cellar, and then at some of the fixed metal shelving. 'We could fasten them to the top shelves, that would stretch their backs a bit. And there's the wire tow-rope in the car.'

'Not bad,' Dawlish said, as if thoughtfully.

'Dawlish, you can't do it,' Tenby gabbled. 'If you beat us up the police would find out, you'd never get away with it. I

—I've told you we didn't intend to kill Mrs. Beresford, we—we pressed harder than we realized, we were horrified to find out that she was dead. We——'

'Which of you killed her?' Dawlish demanded.

Neither man answered.

'All right, Tim,' Dawlish said. 'Go and get that rope from the car——'

'*He killed her!*' Pope gasped, and pointed a quivering finger at Tenby. 'I was in the car when he attacked her. She started to struggle and he pressed too hard.'

Tenby stood rigid, with terror livid on his face.

Dawlish said: 'All right, Tenby. Whose money are you taking for this job?'

'I've told you,' Tenby answered, brokenly. 'I can't do anything more. It's Gorman. You've seen the signatures, you've seen the endowment policies made out to Pope and me, what else do you want? It was Gorman, he's the man you want.'

After another pause, Dawlish said, 'Will you say so in court?'

'Yes,' gasped Tenby. 'Yes, I will!' After a pause, he went on: 'Dawlish, you—you won't hurt my wife, will you? She had nothing to do with it. She—she knew I fiddled a few things, but she wasn't to blame, she never helped me. She—she's a good girl, a good wife, she——'

'Joan Beresford was a good wife,' Dawlish retorted, icily.

Tenby bowed his head.

'As God is my judge, I didn't mean to kill her,' he muttered. 'That wasn't on the cards. I—I'll be honest, Dawlish. I meant to kill you and your wife. That was the idea. Worry you as much as we could, get your nerves raw, and then get rid of you, but—but we didn't plan anything against Mrs. Beresford. We knew Jeremy was in France; we thought if Beresford's wife was missing he would have plenty to think about, and you and your wife would be on your own. That's how we worked it out, Dawlish, I swear it.'

'I almost believe it,' Dawlish said. He turned round and looked at Jeremy, who was taking out a cigarette-case, took a cigarette, lit up, and spoke as the smoke began to trickle through his mouth. 'Think you believe them, Tim?'

'I'd put even money on it.'

Dawlish said: 'I wonder if Tenby knows the names of the women who Gorman swindled. Do you, Tenby?'

'I know some of them. I've got a note of it, in my records, when—whenever I picked up any information like that I just put it down as a small insurance, so I kept a record that no one would suspect. It's in a small red ledger, somewhere at the back: the page marked *Insurance Against Unspecified Loss*. You—you'll see that Mrs. Vaze's name was there once, but I rubbed it out when Gorman was caught. Look for yourself, it's all there.'

Dawlish went to the open safe, looked at the stacked ledgers, found one which answered Tenby's description, and opened it towards the end pages. There was the heading, and there were the entries; seven of them in all. They were all of women, and against each was the figure of a supposed insurance; the highest was seven thousand pounds, the lowest fifteen hundred. Actually, these were the amounts out of which the women had been swindled. By the side of each entry was a name in a column marked *Proposer*—or the swindler. In each case the name was different, but all the names were those which— according to Tenby—Gorman had used as *aliases*.

Was there any reasonable doubt left?

Jeremy asked, 'Satisfied?'

'So far,' Dawlish answered.

'What next?'

'We'll find out whether Pope lives alone next door,' Dawlish said, and turned round on the plump man, who began to talk almost at once.

'I'm a married man with two children, Dawlish. I—I sent the family away until this was over, I didn't want to take any risks with them. There's no one else in the house.'

'Let's go and see,' Dawlish said.

\* \* \* \* \*

There was no one else in 26 Downs Street, but there was one thing in the cellar which nearly broke Dawlish's self-control. In a safe were a dozen of the inflammable containers of nitro-glycerine. Some were quite tiny, but even the smallest was enough to blow a big hole in the wall of a house—and to blow a human body to smithereens.

Pope was free enough with his answers to questions now, admitted that he blackmailed an acquaintance, an industrial chemist, to obtain the explosive and the plastic.

'I ought to put one in your pocket and drop you down the stairs,' Dawlish growled. 'I might, yet.'

'Amen,' Jeremy said, solemnly. 'What's the next job, Pat?'

'We'll go and see Gorman again,' Dawlish answered, 'and when we've checked with him, we'll come back here and

107

hand this pair over to the police. They won't come to any harm if they're left here for a while.'

'Do 'em good,' agreed Jeremy. 'Bread and water every twenty-four hours is about the best they should have. I'll keep them quiet, meanwhile. How did you say they kept Eileen Parish quiet? The adhesive plaster method, wasn't it?'

'Yes,' Dawlish answered, and went on, 'That's a good point.' He looked at Pope. 'Why did you attack Miss Parish?'

Pope hesitated before he answered: 'Gorman told us to rough her up a bit, he said you'd be bound to go and see her, and if you found her being messed about you'd start doubting whether he was really behind it. There isn't a trick Gorman misses, his trouble is that he's too clever.'

Dawlish didn't speak.

'They didn't behave very well to Eileen Parish,' Jeremy said, and looked at the two men owlishly.

'We can leave the refinements until later,' said Dawlish, 'when we know whether they've told the truth or not.'

'Think they have?'

'It sounds like Gorman,' Dawlish admitted, and went on briskly: 'Get a move on, Tim. Tie them up, shut them up, and leave then in the coal dump.'

'Right!' said Jeremy, and sounded as if he were going to enjoy the next ten minutes.

\* \* \* \* \*

In fact it took them fifteen.

Dawlish closed the door of the section of the cellar where the coal was kept, and followed Jeremy up the stairs. They were both grimy from the black dust, and Jeremy had a dark patch on his cheekbone and another under his right eye. He was completely relaxed, and yet there was a bleakness in his eyes and in his voice as he turned into the dining-room, and said:

'Half-way over, Pat. Looks like Gorman all right.'

'I'm still not sure that Chalke's clear,' Dawlish said, evasively, 'and it always has looked too much like Gorman. We've got to make a clean sweep of it, it mustn't start all over again.'

'It's Gorman all right——'

'Oh, he's clever and capable of it all,' Dawlish said, softly. 'The police were fooled, too. He was supposed to be so broke that his sister-in-law paid the premiums on his small insurances and he's worth . . .' He broke off, rubbing the broken bridge of his nose. 'Any man smart enough to do that is smart enough for anything. Tim. Look round and see if you can find a drink, will you?'

'My nose still functions,' Jeremy said, and went straight to a cupboard in a corner behind one of the easy-chairs, opened it, and found that it was fitted out and stocked as a cocktail cabinet. 'As you see,' he added. 'Whisky?'

'Yes.'

'And a splash,' Jeremy said. 'No, I won't drown it. There's one good thing, at least.' He handed Dawlish a glass with two fingers of whisky in it, and held a syphon of soda, poised. 'If we could finish the job tonight, before Ted comes round, it would save a lot of bother.' He squirted for a split second. 'On the other hand,' he added, 'you look as if you could do with some shut-eye.'

'Forget it,' said Dawlish. 'We're going to see Gorman right away.'

'What about Tenby's wife?'

'No reason why she shouldn't sleep in her own bed, now.' Dawlish said. 'There's one more thing I want to check before we see Gorman.'

'Such as?'

'These women whom Tenby named—were they really swindled? The Yard should know,' Dawlish added thoughtfully.

'Our William the Oracle will certainly know,' declared Jeremy. 'All right, Pat. You sit back for five minutes, while I go and produce the buxom body of Claire Tenby. Queer thing,' he added, and paused long enough to finish his drink, then went on as he stepped towards the door: 'Tenby seemed really worried about her, and Pope sent his wife and kids away. How can a man who's fond of his own family do a job like this?'

'Jeremy the Moralist,' Dawlish remarked, and grinned wryly. 'Tim, God knows what I would have done without you. Thanks.' Without a pause, he went on: 'We'll bring Claire in, then we'll go back to the flat, and I'll talk to Trivett from there. I've got to have all the information before I talk to Gorman again, I don't want to allow the slightest chance of being fooled.'

'And you couldn't say fairer than that,' declared Jeremy. He squinted at his watch. 'Close on midnight,' he remarked. 'Trivett might not be too happy about being disturbed. Sure it wouldn't be a good idea to wait until morning?'

'Never more sure,' said Dawlish.

It was past twelve when Jeremy returned, with Claire Tenby draped over his shoulder, fireman fashion. He carried her ahead of Dawlish, up the stairs and into the beautifully appointed bedroom, tumbled her—mink coat and all—on to one of the satin-covered beds, then stood back to look down. 'With ten pounds of fat off she'd be something,' he declared. 'Finished all you want to here?'

'I think so,' Dawlish said.

They closed the door of 28 Downs Street quietly, and then stepped through a slightly thinning fog to the car; Dawlish could make out the glow of the parking lights ten feet away. There was hardly a sound except in the main road, the growling rumble of an engine; a bus was probably leading a convoy of fog-bound cars home. Jeremy took the wheel, and Dawlish did not protest. Visibility was undoubtedly better, although they could not safely travel at more than ten miles an hour, and every corner presented its special problems. They found the main road and, a little after one o'clock, reached Oxford Circus. It was a fairly easy drive down Oxford Street, but the fog became dense again half-way down, and Dawlish said:

'Park her behind the next lot of stranded cars, Tim, and we'll walk the rest.'

'Good idea,' said Jeremy.

Walking was an awkward and slow process, too, but they did not have the feeling of impending calamity every few seconds. Now and again they passed ghostly figures, all carrying flashlights, and one elderly man carrying a candle burning inside a jam-jar. It took them twenty minutes to reach the corner of the mews, but some freak of the fog made it less dense here and they could make out the shape of the three policemen on duty, as well as of a car parked fairly near Beresford's front door; that car hadn't been there when they had left.

'Excuse me, gentlemen!' One of the Yard men came hurrying, shone the torch into their faces, and drew back. 'Sorry, Mr. Dawlish, as I said before, we can't be too sure. There's a lady waiting for you sir. We did not feel justified in allowing her to wait inside the flat.'

'I should think not,' Dawlish said, and his thoughts raced to Felicity. Surely she couldn't have fooled Trivett, couldn't have taken a chance and come here? He stepped out towards the car, saw the door opened by another of the Yard men, and then saw Eileen Parish's long legs as she slid out.

'Mr. Dawlish,' she said, even before she was standing

110

upright, and before Dawlish could utter a word, 'I know just how you feel about the situation, but I can't allow you to take the law into your own hands. Where is my brother-in-law?'

## CHAPTER XIX

## MISSING

DAWLISH could see her clearly, she was so close to him. He could even see the glint in her eyes, the quality of her determination and the fixity of her belief. She did not look at Jeremy, who was just behind him, or at any of the policemen; the only man who mattered to her just then was Dawlish. She moved so that she stood between him and the door, as if she were defying him to pass before he answered her.

He felt a sickening sense of failure as well as acute disappointment. On a night like this, no one could be sure of keeping any man in sight; if Gorman had left Mountjoy Street determined to escape from the police who were watching, he would have no difficulty.

'I know you've had a trying day . . .' Eileen Parish began, 'but——'

Dawlish put a hand firmly on her arm.

'You seem to have had quite a day yourself,' he retorted dryly. 'So he's run away.'

'Where is he, Mr. Dawlish?'

'It's no use asking me,' Dawlish said. 'I don't know. I wish to God I did.' The sickening sense of failure grew much stronger, and his heart began to pound, but he showed no sign of the depth of his feeling as he went on, 'At least I'm glad you're here, I've a few things to tell you about your brother-in-law.' He saw the change in Eileen's expression as she realized that he was telling the truth about not knowing where Gorman was, and she allowed him to lead her towards the flat. Jeremy slipped ahead of them and opened the door. One of the Yard men said:

'I can check with the Yard, sir.'

'Got a radio?'

'Yes, sir, walkie-talkie.'

'Thanks. Will you check?'

Jeremy stood aside as the hall light fell on to Eileen's face and figure. She went ahead of Dawlish, moving with that curious floating grace he had noticed at the house, and even beneath a three-quarter length leopard-skin coat, or perhaps

111

because of it, the magnificence of her figure was remarkable! Dawlish found himself thinking of the moment when he had first seen her, spread-eagled on that bed.

In the big room here, her eyes seemed enormous and very bright, and she looked anxious. She had made up only a little and the lipstick was slightly smeared at one side; everything about her appearance suggested that she had hurried to come here. Beneath the coat she wore a pale-green two-piece, the jacket cut high at the neck and completely concealing the blouse beneath it.

'When did he go?' asked Dawlish.

'It was about seven o'clock,' she answered. 'He had a telephone call. He said . . .' She broke off.

'Well?'

'He said he might as well get it over with. He thought it was from you.'

Dawlish was startled enough to show it.

'Take it easy,' he said. 'He gave you five minutes to choose between us, remember? He wouldn't have come to see me unless I'd dragged him by the hair.'

'I think he would,' Eileen declared, quietly. 'I want to be absolutely honest with you, Mr. Dawlish; he didn't say that it was you, but that was the impression I got. You see, I had been reasoning with him, and he had seen things more clearly.'

Dawlish stared unbelieving.

'I know what you're thinking,' went on Eileen, 'and in some ways you may be right, but I don't believe that any man is really bad. I am quite sure that Maurice was being used as a kind of dummy, or false front, by the people who are really trying to kill you, and I persuaded him to come and talk to you, to try to convince you that he had nothing to do with what had happened. Had it been a fine night, we would have come earlier. After the telephone call, he—well, I've told you what he said. I'm nervous of driving in a fog, I simply couldn't bring myself to take him, and he said he would prefer to walk. He was going to be back at my house by eight o'clock, or he was going to telephone me. When he didn't arrive by ten o'clock, I came here.'

'The fog was still nerve-racking,' Dawlish pointed out.

'I arranged for my garage to send me a driver, and will telephone for another when I'm ready to go home,' Eileen replied. 'What makes you think I am lying to you, Mr. Dawlish?'

112

'I'm trying to make sure,' Dawlish said. 'I haven't caught you out yet, though, have I?' He motioned to a chair. 'Why don't you sit down?'

'How about a drink?' suggested Jeremy, hospitably; he had hardly taken his eyes off Eileen Parish, although she did not appear to have noticed him. 'We can manage pretty well anything.'

She turned to him, as if gratefully, and said: 'I'd love a whisky and water. I got chilled through sitting in the car.'

'Easy as kiss your hand.' Jeremy assured her cheerfully, and as he moved towards the cabinet where the Beresfords kept their drinks, there was a ring at the front-door bell. Dawlish went out of the room, deeply preoccupied. He heard Jeremy introduce himself, and Eileen say that she had guessed who he was. Then Dawlish opened the front door cautiously, keeping to one side as if there was a risk of an assault; but the man who had offered to call the Yard by radio stood there.

'Gorman gave our chaps the slip in the fog, sir,' he announced. 'I can understand it, it's been a hell of a thick night, but you'll be all right provided you stay put.'

Dawlish looked at him blankly.

'If I stay—oh, yes. I see.' A footloose Gorman, a Gorman who might find out what he, Dawlish, knew, might decide that the only way to finish the job he had started was to do it himself. On this particular night it would be easy to move about unseen. Dawlish remembered how vividly he had thought that even while he and the Yard man had been talking in the mews, someone could have crept past them.

Well, no one had. Had they?

'Thanks for being so careful,' Dawlish added and gave a broad but mechanical smile, then closed the door. In the livingroom Eileen Parish was sitting in an easy-chair, well forward on it, knees close together and legs tucked underneath her. She had more colour, and her eyes were very bright; he remembered how they had seemed the colour of chestnuts freshly out of their spiky husk. 'Eileen,' Dawlish said, dryly, 'you have a nasty shock coming to you about your precious brother-in-law.'

'I don't understand you.'

'You will,' Dawlish assured her. 'You paid certain insurance premiums for him while he was in Dartmoor, didn't you?'

'I do have a right to handle my own money the way I think best.'

'That's right,' Dawlish agreed. 'Why did you do it?'

'He was quite without money,' Eileen declared, with her curiously precise diction and choice of word. 'Obviously he would need money when he came out, and I put a little aside for him every month—in fact I also bought him five pounds' worth of Premium Bonds every month. He twice won a hundred pounds in the monthly draw. In addition to this, I kept up payments on his insurances. I knew exactly what I wanted him to do when he came out of prison, but could hardly expect him to do it if he had no money at all, could I?'

'No,' agreed Dawlish. 'But——'

'Let me top that up for you,' Jeremy suggested hospitably. He had always been impressionable, and Eileen Parish was certain to make a good impression on anyone who met her for the first time. How soon her manner and precise diction would become wearisome it was hard to say, but eyes like hers would never tire anyone.

'No, thank you,' Eileen said. 'What are you trying to tell me, Mr. Dawlish?'

'That he's rich. That he robbed a dozen elderly women of their fortunes by making love to them and then swindling them. That all the time he was in Dartmoor he was in touch with the men who have been working against the Beresfords and me. No, don't interrupt,' Dawlish went on, roughly. 'All this is documented and beyond all doubt.' He picked up the red ledger, slapped it, and said: 'He used different names each time, that's why he wasn't caught earlier. For some reason he chose to use his own name with Mrs. Vaze.'

Very slowly Eileen stood up. She held her glass tightly in her left hand. The colour gradually receded from her cheeks. She seemed to square her shoulders as if to brace herself against the shock, and determined that she would not let it knock her too hard.

Dawlish said, 'Do you know where he's gone?'

'No,' she answered, slowly. 'No, I've told you what I thought——' She broke off, and then added in a husky voice, 'Then he might have been lying to me about the telephone call.'

'He probably was,' Dawlish said. 'I'm sorry about this, but you did ask for it. And he's running around loose, so there's no telling when he'll strike next. If there's any way you can help us to find him, you mustn't lose a moment.'

'I won't now,' Eileen promised. She bit her lips, and turned away in a curiously affecting manner. The big chair with the wings seemed to engulf her. Jeremy grimaced at Dawlish. Dawlish looked at the woman for a moment and then moved across the room, sat on the arm of Ted Beresford's chair, and dialled Trivett's home number. He had hardly finished dialling when Trivett answered.

'So you weren't in bed,' Dawlish said.

'I'm in bed, but I've just had a call from the Yard saying that Gorman's got away,' Trivett answered. 'Pat, don't stir out of the flat again tonight. Anything could happen.'

'Anything probably will,' Dawlish said. 'Bill, I want to find out quickly whether certain old ladies I can name were swindled. Who will have the records at the Yard?'

'Tell me who they are, I may remember some of them,' said Trivett.

'Thanks,' Dawlish said. 'The first was a Mrs. Edith Holloway, the second a Miss Maude Evans, another a Mrs. Claude Rochester, yet another a Mrs. Mary Rossetti——'

'That's enough,' Trivett interrupted. 'Three of them ring a bell, and the Rossetti case was a nasty one. She was swindled of all her life's savings by a man who was never identified, and she committed suicide.' After a pause, Trivett went on, 'Are you saying that the man was Gorman?'

'It's beginning to look like it.'

'What have you found? Where have you been?' Trivett almost shouted the words. 'Don't take any chances of losing any evidence. This might be . . .'

He was speaking urgently, and his voice echoed into the room. Jeremy had poured out another whisky-and-soda, and stepped across to Eileen with it, as if he had to do something to ease her mind. She was sitting on the edge of another chair now, staring at Dawlish. Outside, there was the sound of footsteps, as the Yard men took a turn.

That was one split second.

The next, there was a strange kind of gasp, followed by a roar so deafening that it seemed to block their ears. As they moved, instinctively, there was a wild whining sound, then the explosive crack of breaking glass. The curtains billowed into the room, slivers of glass came like arrows and stuck into the wall, the furniture, into the shoulder of Jeremy's coat.

Dawlish felt himself thrown off his chair and pitched on to the floor, still gripping the telephone tightly. He did not see Jeremy fall, or Eileen's chair hurtle along on its castors. The noise was like a cataclysm, with a great roaring outside as well as the fierce red glow of fire. Through all this there was

115

a strangely disembodied voice, Trivett's, calling:

'Are you all right? Pat, are you all right?'

But when Dawlish tried to speak, he could make no sound.

## CHAPTER XX

## HUNT

OUTSIDE, the only noise remaining was the roaring of the fire. As Dawlish staggered to his feet, head reeling, ears singing, he saw through the great rents in the curtains that the old car was blazing, and already it seemed to be a red-hot mass of wreckage. He saw no one moving against the fierce red glow. He heard Trivett's voice, and managed to speak at last:

'Send—send the fire service here. Send——'

'Coming,' Trivett said. 'Don't go away from there.' It seemed a silly thing to say, Dawlish thought vaguely. He put the receiver down slowly, then looked away from the conflagration in the mews, filled with dread for the policemen who had been out there. Next, he saw Eileen on her knees beside Tim Jeremy.

'Oh God!' Dawlish breathed, and stepped towards her, nearly lost his balance, and stood swaying. Outside, some-one was shouting, '*Fire, fire, fire!*' Eileen turned round and looked up into Dawlish's face; there was such distress on hers that Dawlish knew on the instant what he had to fear.

'He's—he's badly hurt,' Eileen said hoarsely. 'A piece of glass stuck—stuck into his neck.'

The jugular, Dawlish thought desperately, and flung him-self forward. Eileen was pressing her thumb over the wound in Jeremy's neck, but the blood was welling up on either side. 'Get a towel. For God's sake hurry!' he shouted. 'Something to pad it with.' He slid his hand round so that his large thumb pressed against the wound. In the single moment that the wound was bare, he saw that it was no more than a quarter of an inch long. The woman scrambled to her feet. It seemed an age before she came back with a face-cloth and a towel, the cloth already padded. Dawlish pressed it tightly on to the wound, and maintained the pressure on that.

'Telephone,' he muttered. '999, ask for ambulance, then . . .'

She had gone.

He heard her speaking into the telephone, saying with that great precision and clearness of mind:

'... Yes, and a blood transfusion will certainly be necessary, the injured man's jugular has been pierced by a splinter of glass.' There were other sounds, including the banging of a door. Dawlish did not look round, but he felt the pounding of fear in his heart.

He heard Eileen catch her breath, and made herself look round, but nothing would make him take his finger away from Jeremy's neck.

He saw a scarecrow of a man, his clothes nearly all blown off, hair burned down to his scalp, eyelashes and eyebrows gone. Only one leg of his trousers remained, and one shoe was blown off. He was clutching his right arm with his left hand. His eyes were unbelievably bright, and when he saw Dawlish, he staggered, and leaned against the wall.

'You—you all right, sir?' he muttered. 'You ...'

Then he fainted and slid down the wall, as Dawlish realized that it was the Scotland Yard man in charge of the mews.

Next Dawlish heard a fire-engine bell, and a few seconds afterwards the shriller ringing of an ambulance bell. He maintained the pressure all the time, looking down at Jeremy's face, which was turned away from him, the mouth slack and the eyes closed; it was almost as if his friend was dead already.

Then the ambulance men and a doctor arrived.

\* \* \* \* \*

When Trivett reached the mews, twenty minutes later, the fire was out except for a smouldering mass of wreckage, some of it still red hot. There was the stench of burning in every corner, and there was fog creeping into the flat through the broken window.

Just before Trivett came in. Tim Jeremy had been taken out of the mews. The ambulance men had also taken the Yard detective. Only Dawlish and Eileen were in the big room, Dawlish dabbing a cut in his forehead; had the glass splinter which had caused that gone half an inch further in, it might have been fatal. There were three small splinters of glass in Eileen's hair, and a slight scratch on the back of her right hand; in the wing of the chair where she had been sitting there were other deadly splinters.

No piece of furniture was untouched, the glass of some pictures was broken, two pictures were on the floor, others

117

were askew on the wall. A great pile of soot had come down the fireplace and spread over the hearth and onto the carpet. Against this Trivett's well-cut, neatly pressed brown suit and shiny hair seemed out of place. He was a good-looking man, usually rather pale, but tanned after a recent holiday in the South of France.

'Tim . . .' Dawlish began.

'I know,' Trivett said. 'I saw him being put into the ambulance. He's got a good chance.'

'He's got a chance in a hundred, if he's lucky,'

'The odds aren't as bad as that,' Trivett insisted. 'There's no need to look on the black side for the sake of it. Do you know how it happened?'

Dawlish didn't speak.

Eileen Parish said, 'I heard some men talking outside, they seemed to think that the explosion was at my car.' The only colour she had was at her eyes. 'Mr. Trivett, do you know if —if anyone outside was badly hurt?'

'One of my men was blown to pieces,' Trivett answered: and beneath his tan, he looked ill. 'One wasn't hurt at all, because he was protected by a doorway. A third is on his way to hospital. There are a few minor casualties in the other flats, through flying glass.' Trivett smoothed down his thick brown hair. 'The explosion could have been caused in any one of three ways. It could have been an explosive thrown from the entrance of the mews, it could have been something in the car, or it could have been something left behind by someone who slipped in through the fog.

Dawlish didn't speak.

'Pat, you've got to keep under cover until this fog has cleared,' Trivett went on. 'You mustn't take another chance of any kind.'

'Is Felicity all right?' Dawlish demanded.

'There isn't the slightest need to worry about Felicity.'

'You'd better mean that,' Dawlish said. He pressed a hand against his head, which was throbbing badly as if men were striking it with hammers. 'What about Gorman? How soon can you pick him up?'

'Certainly not until the fog clears,' Trivett answered. 'And in any case, you ought to have a shot of dope——'

'No shots for me,' Dawlish interrupted. 'I want to be awake when I die. Bill, I've information for you.' He told Trivett exactly what had happened at Downs Road, and what the police would find there, and now and again he glanced across at Eileen, who was sitting back in a small chair looking as if desolation could be no worse. 'So now we know that Gorman was as busy as a bee for years before we caught up with him,' Dawlish went on. 'The signatures on those policies are too definite for there to be any doubt. I think you'll find the description of the men wanted for the other cases tallies fairly well with Gorman's.'

'In height and build, yes,' Trivett said. 'I can remember two or three—the men had different colouring, different characteristics. We checked at the time, as far as we could, but none of the earlier victims was alive. We had three of them see Gorman and hear him speak, but they didn't identify him. He's just about as clever as——'

He broke off.

'That's right,' said Dawlish. 'He hypnotizes people, but he hasn't hypnotized us. Still want to reform him, Miss Parish?' His voice was harsh with bitterness.

Eileen didn't answer.

Trivett said: 'You can't stay here any longer, Pat, you'd better come along to the Yard as we can look after you there. How about you, Miss Parish? Would you rather go back to your house, or stay in a hotel near here?'

After a pause, she looked up and said:

'I'll go home, please, Superintendent.' She stood up as if the movement was a considerable effort, and came across to Dawlish. 'I can't tell you how desperately sorry I am,' she declared. 'There is nothing—nothing at all—that I would not do to make amends.'

'If you hear from your brother-in-law,' Dawlish said, 'just let me know.'

'I——' She broke off, bit her lips, and turned away. Trivett went with her to the door, and Dawlish heard him giving instructions to one of his men to drive her home. Soon, the engine of a car sounded. Trivett came back into the flat, looked around, and said:

'It's a shambles. You were lucky to get away with it.'

'Yes,' said Dawlish bleakly. 'Lucky is the word, Bill, that bomb—we've got to find out how it was delivered. We mustn't lose a minute.'

'We're doing everything we possibly can,' Trivett told him. 'You can't do a thing more. Come along to the Yard, and——'

'Believe it or not, the bedrooms aren't touched,' Dawlish said. 'I'm staying on the premises. Presumably no one will make any further attempt to get past the police here.' The bitterness in his voice had a weary note. 'I'll put my head down for a few hours, Bill, and see you in the morning.'

After a long pause, Trivett said, 'I suppose it's no use arguing with you.' He nodded, turned towards the door, looked back and said, 'Pat, it isn't any use trying to say what I think.'

'You look after Felicity,' Dawlish said gruffly. 'That's your one and only job so far as I'm concerned. Thanks, Bill. Will you arrange an hourly inquiry at the hospital from the Yard ?'

'Yes.'

'I'll call them when I've had a few hours' rest,' Dawlish said, and added in a high-pitched note, '*Rest!*'

He went into the spare room of the flat, across a small passage from the Beresford's room. He and Felicity had used this flat for their honeymoon, and had often spent a night here since. Felicity, Felicity, Joan, Ted—Tim. This place was peopled by ghosts of the living and by ghosts of the dead. Perhaps Trivett had been right, perhaps it had been a mistake to stay here. He would never go to sleep, could not even doze, while these ghosts surrounded him. Joan and Tim. He felt almost certain that Jeremy would not recover from this wound; and if he died, then Gorman . . .

Dawlish gritted his teeth.

Then he thought: 'There's only one way to beat Gorman, and that's to out-think him. He's bound to try for me again.' He lay with his eyes closing, on his back, warm beneath the two eiderdowns, hearing occasional sounds but none of them loud enough to disturb him. He could almost claim that he hadn't done too badly. But for Joan, but for Tim, he would have felt that he was doing well. At least, he knew the answer now.

*Did* he?

He turned over on his side and screwed up his eyes. That needle of doubt remained. Why? He found himself back in the house in Downs Road, hearing Tenby's statement, and, later, hearing Pope's. Had they talked too freely? They had been prodded by terror, of course, and probably he did not know how murderous he had looked, but—why had they poured out *every*thing? Was he right in believing that Chalke was completely free from suspicion, just because they said he was? Chalke was a man of influence and power. Chalke had put a lot of business in Tenby's way. He, Dawlish, had been so determined to believe that Gorman was the man that he had been too easily put off Chalke.

Why not Chalke *and* Gorman?

Was that possible? Tenby and Pope must have known that they had no chance of escaping from the police or from Dawlish, and each man was fond of his wife, Pope was fond of his wife and children. If they were going to prison for a long time, knowing that they were facing life sentences, each would want to make sure that his wife and family was looked after. By being loyal to Chalke, they might assure that; by naming him, they might be condemning their families to penury as well as to shame.

So—the obvious thing for them to do was to point a finger at Gorman.

Yet there were the insurance policies, and the other irrefutable evidence that Gorman had a fortune, that he had worked with both Tenby and Pope.

Had it been a mistake to tell Trivett about the two men? If he had said nothing, and visited them again in the morning, he would have had a better chance of judging whether they had kept anything back. Once under charge from the police, they would lie with impunity. It might take some time for the truth to come out—for instance, it would be worth knowing who was likely to pay for their defence. But he couldn't afford to wait. The danger hovered over and about him, as the fog and smog hovered about the city; and each could kill.

He thought of Tim Jeremy.

Then, blessedly, he fell asleep.

\* \* \* \* \*

He woke to a confusion of sounds and of voices, and lay on his side, remembering on the instant where he was and what had happened, seeing the small window of this room with the curtains drawn back, as if someone had been in here. Then he distinguished one of the voices quite clearly, and exclaimed aloud, 'Ted!'

He pushed the bedclothes back, and got out of bed. He was stiff; the buffet from the explosion and the fall in St. Martin's Lane had done more damage than he had realized, and he grunted as he straightened up. He reached the door of the living-room, and saw Ted Beresford standing with his back to the window, looking at Eileen Parish. She was bright-eyed, and well made-up, her smooth complexion flawless; somehow, she did not look quite real, and he realized that she had on too much powder. She wore a simply cut suit of clerical grey, and a white silk blouse with ruffles at the neck.

Neither she nor Beresford had heard Dawlish come in, and Beresford was saying:

'There isn't any need to blame yourself, Miss Parish.'

'All we want is Gorman,' Dawlish said loudly, and the others swung round.

Beresford's eyes still seemed to burn, but he was obviously much more rested. He hadn't shaved, and the dark, greying stubble made the deep lines at his mouth and chin look deeper and more craggy. Dawlish had a strange impression; that Ted would never be able to laugh again.

'Hallo, Pat,' he said quietly.

'Hallo, Ted,' Dawlish said, 'Any news of Tim?'

In the moment that he waited, he felt a kind of terror, in case the news was bad. Then Ted said:

'I talked to Trivett half an hour ago. Tim got through the night, so his chances are a lot better.'

Dawlish said, 'Thanks.' He pushed a hand through his hair, looked at Eileen, and asked, 'What brought you so early?'

'Early?' she looked startled. 'It's past eleven.'

'Good God!' Dawlish was shaken into exclaiming.

'I can tell you what brought her,' Ted declared in a hard voice. 'She seems to have decided that if we tackle Gorman ourselves we shall be condemning ourselves to eternal damnation. This, she insists, is a matter for the police, and we mustn't soil our hands on her brother-in-law's neck. Tell her that she's wasting her time, will you?'

'Mr. Dawlish, I know how you both feel, I know how terrible it is, and I know how dreadfully wrong I've been,' Eileen said, and her hands were stretched out as if in supplication. 'But it doesn't alter the fact that if you take the law into your own hands, you will be committing a crime, and you might even regret it for the rest of your lives. It's a matter only for the police.'

After a long pause, Beresford growled: 'It's a matter for us, never mind the police. You know where he is, don't you?'

Eileen Parish did not answer.

## CHAPTER XXI

# BETRAYAL?

THE pause lengthened, Beresford was staring fixedly into Eileen's eyes, and she did not look away from him. Dawlish studied them closely, sensing the clash and the struggle between them. The woman was right, of course, in every way she was right, but—wasn't Beresford right, too?'

Beresford said roughly: 'She knows. Where is he?'

Eileen didn't answer.

Dawlish said, in an unexpectedly mild voice, 'Have you told the police where to find him?'

She still didn't answer.

'Eileen,' Dawlish went on, as if with an effort, 'I'll go all the way with you about it being a job for the police and not for us, but the police must be told where he is. Do you know?'

'No,' Eileen said at last. She reminded Dawlish of the way she had looked last night, when she had turned round from Tim Jeremy, pressing her finger on that little, deadly wound. Her eyes had the same brightness, as of agony, and her face the same pallor. 'No,' she repeated, 'but he telephoned only this morning and he promised to call again at five o'clock this evening. I asked him to call this number—it's in the directory—and said I would be here. Then you'll be able to hear me, and at least you'll know that I've *tried* to make him stop this awful thing.'

'There's just one way to stop him,' said Beresford very calmly. 'That is, by breaking his neck. Or better still, strangling him.' His eyes were burning, his hands raised a little in front of him, the fingers crooked; Dawlish remembered being like that and feeling like that—only yesterday, only a few hours ago. He watched the two of them intently, and was especially aware of the glitter in the woman's eyes. 'Remember what happened to my wife? Remember how she was attacked on the way home? Remember she was a happy woman, she was a good woman, she—God! You make me sick!'

'I'm going to try to stop him,' Eileen replied huskily. 'I can't do more than that. The important thing . . .' When she turned to Dawlish there was a throb of appeal in her voice: 'The important thing is that neither of you should have a chance to kill him. You would regret it all your lives. I came to ask you to leave London until the police have found out the whole truth. Maurice can't do any more harm now.'

'She would like to see us run,' Beresford sneered. He dropped his arms. 'I'll be here at one o'clock,' he went on. 'I hope you'll try hard.'

Eileen looked at Dawlish.

Dawlish said, 'If you know where your brother-in-law is, and don't tell the police, you'll be responsible for anything else that happens.'

'I've got to try to reason with him,' she insisted. 'I'm sorry.' She moved slowly towards the door, hesitated, looked as if she was going to turn round and speak again, but went out. A man at the front door spoke to her, but she didn't answer. Beresford went to the window, which had been covered on the outside with a large sheet of transparent plastic, and gave a blurred view of the mews.

'She's the kind that would die at the stake,' he said. 'If you hadn't been here . . .' He swung round from the window. 'She knows where he is, of course.'

'She might do.'

'Pat——'

'Ted,' Dawlish interrupted, 'if we get on to Gorman's trail, if we find him, if he puts up a fight, if you break his neck—no one is going to blame you. But whatever we think about it and whatever we've done in the past, Eileen Parish is absolutely right: Gorman is a job for the police. I'll tell Trivett what we think, and he won't make any mistakes.'

Beresford looked at him through narrowed eyes, then shrugged, and said:

'I think you're crazy. But . . .' He seemed to grit his teeth. 'I've got things to do. I've got to see the undertaker. I've got to see a printer and a florist.' He stood very still. 'Joan's mother had a stroke when she heard the news, that's why I couldn't come back straight away. I'll go and get things moving. How long will you be getting ready?'

'Half an hour.'

'I'll be back in an hour,' Beresford promised. He turned and went out, and Dawlish watched his massive figure pass through the doorway leading to the passage and the front door, yet Beresford's strong, craggy face still seemed to be in the room. Dawlish went into the kitchen, made himself some tea, and belatedly began to marvel that he had slept for so long. Apart from the heavy blanket of depression he felt much more himself.

There was the added complication now: of Ted.

Ted wasn't going to see the undertaker, the printer or the florist. Ted was going to see Eileen Parish, to try to force her to tell where Gorman was. Perhaps that had to be done. If she had promised to tell the police he could have dealt with Ted, but not now; at least, not yet.

Dawlish had a shave and a shower, made some toast, and in half an hour, was dressed in an old suit which he kept at the flat for emergency use. He still felt fairly fit and fresh, apart from the stiffness and that had nearly worn off.

As he was about to leave, the telephone-bell rang. He answered it reluctantly, and a girl said:

'This is New Scotland Yard, Mr. Trivett wants you,' and left him holding the instrument for what seemed a long time. Dawlish stood staring about the room. It wouldn't be long before someone would have to start tidying it up; that might be one of the things Trivett wanted. Then he saw that Eileen Parish had left her handbag, tucked by the side of a chair. It was of brown crocodile, brightly polished, and it reminded him of her eyes. To have left that, she must have been worked up. Well, that had been very apparent.

'Pat?' Trivett said at last.

'Yes,'

'Sorry to keep you,' Trivett went on. 'There was a report that Gorman had been seen at London Airport, but it was someone who looked like him. Have you seen Ted?'

'Yes.'

'Can't you keep him off Gorman?'

'No.'

'Pat, it isn't going to help anyone if Ted finds Gorman and kills him,' said Trivett, earnestly. 'He's said a dozen times that he won't rest until he's broken Gorman's neck. He would never get away with it as self-defence. I told you at the beginning of this that you would have to be careful with Ted.'

'I'll be careful,' Dawlish promised. 'Have you seen Tenby and Pope?'

'Yes,' answered Trivett. 'I've found also more of the nitro-glycerine in the cellar. There isn't any doubt that they took Miss Parish's car, that they kidnapped Joan and strangled her, and that they put Ted's telephone line out of order. We now know that Pope drove through the night to get to Exeter the next morning so that he could telephone you from there. Then he drove straight back to London. They both swear that Gorman is the principal. I've had a handwriting expert on the signatures to those endowment policies, and there isn't any doubt that they were all written by Gorman. With endowments alone, all due to mature within a year and most of them overdue, Gorman is worth over fifty thousand pounds. He made a mistake in using the same aliases for his swindling jobs as for some of his insurances, he must have felt too sure of himself. They all do,' Trivett added, heavily. 'I doubt if we've evidence enough to prove that he was the man who swindled the other women, unless one or two are still alive and can identify him—but he specialized in the very old persons. There is a coincidence of dates between the time they were swindled and the taking out of fresh policies, too. He had several different names, as you know, and rented furnished rooms under several of them. He did the job thoroughly and if it hadn't been for you he might have got away with it. The Vaze job was to be his last one.'

'Don't tell me you believe that,' Dawlish said sceptically.

'I believe it because of papers which we've found at Tenby's place,' Trivett answered. 'We haven't been through them all yet, but there's a lot of evidence that Gorman was closing down his operations. Tenby says it was because of his son. Gorman was planning to leave the country, and everything was set. Mrs. Tenby says that she knew Gorman at the time, and that Gorman said that he had been influenced by his sister-in-law—he was going to get out so that he needn't bring his son into the game. He was well enough off to retire, anyhow. There's some story that the boy found out, and instead of being shocked, was intrigued by it, and wanted to take part in the last job.'

Dawlish said quietly, 'I see, Bill.'

'You can also see that it would make Gorman even more bitter,' Trivett went on. 'Claire Tenby says that he was absolutely on top of the world, she'd never known him happier since his marriage. There could be more in Eileen Parish's notions than we like to think.'

'I see, Bill. What else did Tenby and Pope say?'

'Not much,' Trivett replied. 'They're still answering questions, but the background picture remains the same. So does our big problem—making sure that Ted doesn't kill Gorman. Where is he now?'

'Attending to some of the formalities,' Dawlish answered. 'Aren't you having him followed?'

'You know as well as I do that if Ted wants to slip our chaps, he can.'

'Yes,' agreed Dawlish, and after a pause, he added quietly: 'All right, Bill. I'll look after him.' He rang off, hesitated, leaned forward and picked up the shiny crocodile handbag. tucked it under his arm, and then went out. A wrecker's van was at the entrance to the mews, laden with most of the debris from the burnt-out Austin, and three policemen were on duty. The walls of the mews were smoke blackened, and there seemed hardly a whole window left in sight.

Dawlish pushed his way through towards the street, and found his Allard parked where he had left it. He also saw two Yard men in a car just behind him. He waved, gave them time to start their engine, and for the first five minutes made sure that they found it easy to trail him. By that time, they would take it for granted that he was going to co-operate. As he turned into Piccadilly from Bruton Street, he accelerated fiercely, cut in front of the nose of a bus, swung towards Piccadilly, and left the police car standing. It could not hope to guess which road he took at Hyde Park Corner, and there was a stream of traffic holding it up at the intersection. He slackened his pace, and drove towards Chelsea, and Mount-joy Street. He left his car in a street nearby, got out, and approached Eileen Parish's home. He saw two plain-clothes men watching; but they would not be troubled or surprised to see him. They were on the look-out only for Gorman and for strangers. He beckoned one of the men, whom he recognized, and as the man came up, he asked briskly:

'Is Miss Parish home?'

'Yes, sir. She arrived about an hour ago.'

'By herself?'

'Mr. Beresford arrived about half an hour afterwards,' the Yard man said. 'I report hourly, sir, and that's due to go in my next report—in twenty minutes' time.'

'That's fine,' said Dawlish. 'I expect we'll both be out by then.' He gave a bleak smile, and went towards the house.

CHAPTER XXII

KILL?

As HE turned into the gateway, Dawlish looked across the road, and saw the curious neighbour at her window; that didn't surprise him. He remembered vividly how he had forced the door of this house before under the woman's eyes. He saw that a new Yale lock had been fitted; the police had arranged that quickly. He opened Eileen's bag, standing with his back to the street so that no one could see what he was doing.

Inside were the usual oddments: a folded handkerchief, a lipstick, a flapjack, a small purse, two keys including one which was obviously very new, and a little square, leather article he didn't recognize. He picked this up, saw that it folded in two on a small hinge, opened it and found a small travelling clock, the newest alarm kind, with the red alarm hand set for six o'clock. It was going, but the tick was so silent that it could hardly be heard. Everything about the bag and the contents was of the finest quality, and hardly used. He put the watch back carefully, took the new key, slid it into the lock, and pushed the door back. He paused for a moment, as if speaking to someone who had opened the door, then stepped inside. He closed the door softly.

He listened intently, but heard nothing.

Holding the bag in his right hand, he stepped towards the stairs and strained his ears to catch the slightest sound; he heard none. He crept up the stairs, looked into the rooms on the first floor; all the doors were open, a coat—the one which Eileen had been wearing at the flat—was flung over the foot of the bed, but there was no sign of her or Beresford. Tight-lipped, Dawlish went up to the next floor, and all the rooms there were empty, too.

He murmured, 'Cellar?'

He made little sound as he hurried down the stairs and into the other rooms on the ground floor; as these were empty, the cellar was the only place left. Perhaps it had been the obvious place, anyhow, for sounds from the cellar were not likely to be heard so easily anywhere else. He found a door not unlike the one at Downs Road—the two houses had something in common, having been built about the same period. He stepped to the top of a flight of wooden stairs, and then heard a gasp.

A rumble of a man's voice followed.

'Ted,' Dawlish said, *sotto voce*. 'Ted, you bloody fool.' He crept down the wooden stairs, keeping close to the wall so as to lessen the risk of creaking. As he reached the foot, he heard a woman cry out, as if in pain. He saw a sliver of light, through a partly open door—a door to his left, and away from the front of the house.

Beresford said, in that hard, grating voice which seemed to have been born with the news of what had happened to Joan:

'You can stop this the moment you want to. Where is Gorman?'

'I—I've told you I don't know,' Eileen gasped. 'I've told you I don't know!' ..

'And I've told you I know you're lying,' Beresford answered.

Dawlish pushed the door open a little wider, his teeth gritting together. In the years that were past he and Ted together had used harsh, even brutal tactics to get what information they needed; in the days of the Resistance in France one hadn't been squeamish, and with men like Tenby and Pope one wasn't squeamish. But this ...

He saw Beresford with his back towards him, a huge, towering, menacing figure. He saw Eileen, sitting on an upright chair—if 'sitting' was the right word. She was crouching, and leaning forward. Beresford had her left wrist in his right hand, and was pushing her arm backwards, twisted at an angle which he knew created agonizing pain. She was fully dressed; Beresford hadn't lost his head completely. And there was something about the way he was standing which told Dawlish the truth: that he, Beresford, hated this. He was forcing himself to use the pressure, but if Eileen didn't give way soon, he would probably stop. Dawlish remembered the way he had looked when he had said, '*She's the kind who would die at the stake.*' There was a beading of sweat on her forehead, and her eyes seemed to glisten with pain.

'And I've told you that it won't take much more to break your arm,' Beresford said, with a kind of restrained savagery. 'Don't blame me. Where is Gorman?'

'Oh dear God!' Eileen gasped. 'I can't stand any more, God forgive me. He—he's coming here at two o'clock.'

\* \* \* \* \*

Beresford let her go.

Dawlish stood in the doorway, able to see them both clearly, but only visible if they stared straight at the partly open door. Ted moved to one side, wiping his forehead with the back of his hand; undoubtedly he had been near breaking point, too. Dawlish wondered how far he would have gone, but that didn't matter now; he had the answer he wanted.

Beresford was breathing hard. Eileen was leaning back on the chair, as if in an attitude of complete exhaustion. Her lips moved, and Dawlish thought he lip-read, '*God forgive me, God forgive me.*' Beresford fumbled in his pocket, took out a cigarette-case, lit a cigarette, and stood staring at his victim.

'If he'll be here at two o'clock,' he said, 'what was that line about him telephoning to my flat?'

She didn't answer.

'You mustn't get anything wrong,' Beresford said. 'I can start all over again.'

She moistened her lips.

'I—I was going to try to make him come with me,' she answered. 'I wanted to make sure you would both be there at five o'clock. I can't help what has happened. I still believe that—that you're wrong about him. I don't believe he would have anything to do with murder! I—I believed I could persuade him to come with me, and—and I was sure he could telephone.' She broke off again, and asked piteously, 'Can I —can I have a drink of water?'

'In a minute,' Beresford answered. 'What made you think he might come in person?'

'Can't you understand?' gasped Eileen. 'He's a hunted man. Ever since your wife died he's been on the run. The very moment he stepped out of the prison gates he's been in awful danger. He can't know which way to turn. Even if— even if you're right, even if he did have anything to do with planning these crimes, he still doesn't know which way to turn. And—and I was going to make sure the police knew he was coming, there wouldn't have been any danger to him from you.'

'No,' Beresford said, thinly. 'No, there wouldn't. Two o'clock, you say.'

'Yes, he . . .' Eileen hesitated, then slid forward in her chair, and for a moment it looked as if she were going to fall down on her knees in front of Beresford. 'You mustn't kill him. A life for a life won't do any good, and—and you would be branded with it for ever.'

'It's the kind of brand I'd be proud of,' Beresford growled. 'You can get up.' He stood back as she did so, awkwardly. 'We've still got an hour, there's no reason why you shouldn't go upstairs for part of the time.' She staggered, and he took her arm roughly. 'Don't try to put it on, you're not hurt,' he said.

Then he saw Dawlish.

Eileen saw him at the same time.

They stood quite still, Beresford and the woman staring at

Dawlish, the woman taking in short, shallow breaths; Beresford hardly seemed to be breathing at all, and it was a long time before Dawlish said, quite equably:

'Hallo, Ted.'

'Fancy seeing you,' rejoined Beresford, with a futile attempt at being flippant. 'You can walk through brick walls now, can you?' He wiped his forehead again. 'How long have you been here?'

'Long enough,' answered Dawlish. 'Come on, Eileen.' He moved quickly, lifted her off her feet, and carried her up the stairs briskly, taking two steps at a time and not caring how much noise he made. He took her along to the immaculate red-and-black kitchen, where there was a modern type of armchair; he sat her in this, then went to the sink and poured out a glass of water. Beresford had followed, and stood in the doorway, his face expressionless, his body relaxed.

Dawlish put the glass to Eileen's lips and she held her head back and sipped a little. As soon as he took the glass away, she said tensely:

'Don't let him kill Maurice.'

'You know, you could have misjudged me,' said Dawlish easily. 'I might be as anxious to settle this personally as Ted Beresford is. I don't think your precious brother-in-law could be convicted of murder. His counsel would claim that he hadn't intended murder and gave no instructions—that the murder was committed only by Tenby and Pope. Right, Ted?'

'Right,' said Beresford, and his eyes began to glow.

'And if that were so, Gorman might only get a comparatively short prison sentence. Seven years, say. That wouldn't be any satisfaction to us, would it, Ted?'

'No,' Beresford agreed harshly.

'We want to make sure that he dies,' Dawlish went on.

Eileen was leaning back, her eyes closed, her hands clasped in front of her, an expression of utter despair in her face. Except for her shallow breathing, she made no sound. Dawlish glanced round at Beresford, who was coming forward slowly. He was staring at the woman, and there was no compassion in his eyes; Dawlish had a momentary recollection of the way Tim Jeremy had looked at her.

Beresford drew alongside.

'Pat,' he said, without a change of tone, 'I'm sorry about this.' He swung his right arm, the fist tightly clenched, in a terrific blow at Dawlish's stomach, perfectly judged for the

131

solar plexus. Dawlish, taken completely by surprise, felt a screaming vortex of pain at the nerve centres. His legs crumpled up, as if he were paralysed. He felt himself held by Beresford, and half-dragged across the room, then propped up in a chair. He heard Eileen scream. He could not see her, the tears of pain in his eyes made a shimmer of silver, that was all; he could not even lift his hand. Through the roaring in his ears he heard sounds which might have been the woman, screaming, but there was nothing he could do about it, his whole body was in agony, and there was no strength in him.

* * * * *

Beresford said, 'I'm sorry about this,' and realized that Dawlish was completely unaware of what was going to happen; and then hit him. He saw the anguish which twisted his friend's face, stopped him from falling, and supported him to a chair. As he did so, he said in a hard voice: 'I've got to get Gorman, Pat, and you would stop me. I've worked with you too long to be fooled.'

Then Eileen Parish screamed, and sprang up from her chair. Beresford swung round from Dawlish as the woman neared the door which led into the garden. He stretched out his long arms, clutched her dress, and hauled her back; before she could cry out again, he clapped his hand over her mouth. He put his left arm round her, hoisted her off the floor and, hugging her close to his body, limped across to the sink and pulled a tea-towel off a hook. He kept his right hand over her mouth all the time, twisted the cloth round clumsily so that it made a kind of rope, then removed his hand from her mouth. She drew in a shuddering squeaking breath, and was about to scream as he swung the tea-towel over her head and drew it tight round her mouth, gagging her. She made a gurgling sound. He drew the cloth tight, tied a double knot, and let her go. She staggered away from him.

He looked at Dawlish, who was conscious but obviously in pain, and as obviously almost paralysed. He was leaning forward, arms folded across his stomach. and Beresford knew that he was trying to squeeze the pain away. Eileen was leaning helplessly against the sink. Beresford glanced at the windows, made sure no one was approaching and that no one had seen what had happened, and then lifted the woman and dumped her back into her chair. He saw an apron with long strings hanging behind the door, put this round her and the back of the chair, and tied it behind her. She could not get up, and it would take her a long time to tear the tapes.

He stepped towards Dawlish, who seemed to be trying to draw in breath, and he said again: 'Sorry, Pat, but this is my job. No one else owes Gorman as much as I do, and you're right, you know: the police probably couldn't prove murder against him.' He paused, and then went on talking to himself. 'I didn't think the time would come when I'd have to do this to you. At least I fooled you. I've learned something over the years. I wonder what you would feel if Gorman had killed Felicity. I wonder if you would thank me for stopping you from killing him?'

Dawlish gave a sound which was between a gasp and a groan.

'I wish I had a hypo by me and could give you a jab,' Beresford said, calmly. 'The only way I can put you to sleep is by . . .'

He raised his hand, as if he were going to bring it down savagely on the back of Dawlish's neck; but as he did so he heard a sound along the passage. A moment later a footstep of a man coming towards this room. Beresford swung round from Dawlish in a flash, and peered through the crack between the door and the framework.

Gorman was only a few feet away from him.

CHAPTER XXIII

# KILLER

DAWLISH knew what was going on.

He could hear and he could see, although through a blur, and every now and again the blur became opaque. He saw Eileen sitting helplessly in a chair close by him, and Ted straightening up from him, Dawlish, as if he were startled. He heard everything that Ted said, and understood exactly what he intended to do. Then he had a moment's reprise, for Ted swung away and went to the door.

Someone was coming, then. Someone . . .

The door was thrust open wide, and Gorman came in.

At that moment Dawlish's vision was uninterrupted. He saw the change of expression on Gorman's face, first of astonishment, then of sheer horror. Gorman gaped first at his sister-in-law, then at Dawlish. The next moment Beresford put out a hand, gripped his wrist and dragged him bodily into the kitchen. He struck him savagely beneath the chin, and the blow seemed like the crack of a whip. Dawlish's vision blurred, it was almost as if the blow had been landing on him. He saw Gorman reeling drunkenly towards the sink, then collapse, knocked out. He expected Beresford to keep hitting the man, but instead Beresford went out of the room; his footsteps sounded heavy, light, heavy, light. Different sounds followed, and Dawlish realized that the bolts were being shot home; Beresford was making sure that no one could come and interrupt.

Before Beresford got back, Gorman was conscious again, on his knees, and pulling at a drawer in a cupboard at one side of the sink. Knives and forks rattled, tinnily. Gorman was gasping for breath, and holding on to the sink with one hand while he pulled. The drawer jolted open, and nearly fell, but stayed at a drunken angle. Beresford's footsteps sounded again—heavy, light, heavy, light. He came in as Gorman pulled a carving knife from the drawer, and numbed as he was, Dawlish felt the desperation in the man, as well as the quickness of his mind. Gorman was still crouching, half-dazed, but held the knife with his thumb on the upper part of the handle. If Beresford came towards him, he could stab forward and upwards.

He stood, glaring defiance.

'Oh, no,' Beresford said, and it seemed to Dawlish that there was a savage edge of laughter in his voice, as if this were a moment that he was actually enjoying. He had been prepared for it, of course. 'You wouldn't try to cut my throat, or stick my ribs, would you? Anyone trying to do that must have his neck broken.' He lunged forward, on his sound left leg. Gorman made a thrust, Beresford swung his good leg up and kicked the knife out of Gorman's grasp. 'You wouldn't take advantage of a one-legged man, would you?' Beresford stood grinning and glaring at Gorman, and Dawlish knew what he had feared from the moment he had heard the news: that the death of Joan had turned Ted Beresford's head until he was not truly sane. 'Gorman,' Beresford went on in his grating voice, 'I am now coming to put my hands round your neck. I am going to choke the life out of you, and I am going to do it slowly. So that it hurts. So that you know what's happening to you. So that you know just how my wife felt when your hired thugs attacked her. Understand?

Gorman tried to dodge to one side. Beresford clutched his right arm, drew him close, and then threw him back against

134

the sink. The force with which Gorman struck it must have caused great pain. He gasped, and stayed there, gaping at Beresford, seeing how Beresford's hands were stretched towards him. All the time Dawlish was trying to get one word out, one sentence, which would stop Beresford.

He tried; but he could not speak.

He saw Gorman dodge again, only to be dragged back with the same savage ruthlessness. Then Beresford's big body hid the smaller man. Dawlish saw from the way Beresford's shoulders were hunched that he now had his hands round Gorman's neck, knew that it could only be a matter of seconds.

Dawlish tried to cry out again, and a husky sound came, the kind of sound one would make in a nightmare. He drew in his breath, bringing excruciating pain to his chest and stomach. He saw Beresford's shoulders moving as if he were not only choking but shaking Gorman.

'*He didn't do it!*' Dawlish managed to cry, and he prayed that the words would reach Beresford's ears. '*He didn't do it!*'

Beresford's shoulders seemed to stop moving and for a moment there was only silent stillness. At last Beresford turned slowly round, one arm holding Gorman by the throat. His eyes held the glitter which Dawlish had seen in them too often, and his lips were writhing.

'*It—wasn't—Gorman,*' Dawlish gasped.

'What the hell do you mean, it wasn't Gorman?' grated Beresford. 'Don't give me that. Don't try to stop me. This is my job.'

'Gorman didn't plan it,' Dawlish gasped, and clutched at his neck, stretched it upwards, looked towards the sink. 'Gimme—some water.' He tried to sit up but could not, and he wondered if any other man in the world could strike such a paralysing blow as Beresford had struck him. He watched Beresford hesitate, then saw him release Gorman, who slid down to the floor. Beresford half filled a glass, came over, and rasped:

'Don't fool me. Don't even think you can fool me. I know what I'm doing. If it wasn't Gorman, who was it?'

Dawlish grabbed the glass, spilled water over his hand and over his lap, thrust the glass to his lips and drank, gasped for breath, dropped the glass, and then looked across at Eileen Parish.

'She planned it,' he answered, between gasps. 'Eileen Parish planned it.'

Dawlish did not know whether his voice carried to the woman or not, and he stared at her, and then went on to Beresford. 'Take—take the handbag out of my pocket.' He leaned to one side, and as Beresford put his hand down, he added urgently, '*Be careful!*' Beresford took the handbag out, and handed it to Dawlish, who looked across at Eileen Parish.

Now she knew what he was doing, even if she hadn't heard what he said.

'Pat . . .' Beresford began. 'If you're lying to save Gorman——'

'Watch—this,' gasped Dawlish, and made as if to toss the handbag across the room.

As he drew it back, the woman made a desperate effort to get up from the chair, and terror flared up in her eyes. Dawlish drew the bag back. 'In there, Ted,' he managed to say, 'there is a time bomb. Nitro-glycerine inside a little alarm clock. No doubt specially packed to stand ordinary movement, but ready to blow up at the tick of the right second, or on violent impact. Timed for six o'clock—when you and I and possibly Gorman were supposed to be at the mews.' He paused, fighting for breath, while both of them stared at him. Then he went on: 'She brought that to the mews last night. She knew when it would go off, and changed her chair when she knew it was about to explode. It was timed. I think that first . . .' He broke off, with a wheezy, grating cough, and before he could speak again there was a sharp knock at the front door. Almost at once there were footsteps in the garden, and he managed to say: 'Release her, Ted. Don't let the police find you——'

* * * * *

When the police came in, admitted both at the back and front by Beresford, Eileen Parish was no longer bound to the chair. When Trivett arrived, fifteen minutes later, summoned by the watching police the moment Gorman had been seen to arrive, Dawlish was feeling stiff but free from acute pain. Gorman was conscious, but his neck and chin were badly bruised. Eileen Parish was sitting in the front room, as silent as she had been from the moment Dawlish had pretended to throw the handbag at her.

'Bill,' Dawlish said, 'we can worry about the reasons for it later. I can only guess at them. But plenty of facts add up to the right answer—that Eileen Parish was behind all this.' He pointed to the travelling clock, opened now, and revealing the flat pack of nitro-glycerine which would have killed them all had it exploded in the big room of the mews flat.

'What facts?' asked Trivett.

'Mind going back to the beginning, and the first doubt about Gorman's complicity?' Dawlish said. 'Would Gorman be fool enough to start this campaign at that particular time? If he were crazy, perhaps—and the seven years of brooding over the loss of his son would have turned him mad. But if he were sane—and the letter from the prison chaplain suggested that he was not only sane but ready to admit that trying to avenge his son wasn't worth while—then there had to be some other explanation.'

Trivett nodded. Two Yard men were watching Dawlish, as if fascinated. Beresford was leaning back against a cabinet, glancing from time to time at the woman; he seemed to have aged many years in the last half-hour. Gorman was sitting on a pouffe, elbows on his knees, staring fixedly at Dawlish.

'We were being forced to suspect Gorman,' Dawlish went on. 'The timing, the telephone call, even when I gave the man who phoned a message from Exeter a message for Gorman, every indication pointed to him, but—I began to wonder if it could be someone else. So two things had to be attempted, Bill. First, find out who might be doing it, and second, find out who was pointing guilt at Gorman.'

'Eileen Parish was, for one.'

'Everything she said made it look worse for Gorman, once I probed her statements, I doubt whether I would have started wondering about her so early but for finding her stripped and spread-eagled on her own bed. It was a stagy piece of work altogether—far too stagy. She wasn't really hurt. Even the adhesive plaster wasn't pressed tightly down on to her lips. Quite soon after she was off the bed she could move about without difficulty; why would men who had strangled Joan be so gentle with another woman? There was a possible answer from Tenby—that Gorman had laid it on to try to hoodwink me, but if Gorman hadn't laid it on, who had? Someone who was trying to hoodwink me, of course, and who knew I would be at the house. No one could know, they could only guess—unless they knew I was on the way. For instance, supposing I was followed, supposing my route made it obvious where I was going, supposing my trailer telephoned here and passed on the news. One man and a willing victim could lay on the strip-tease and gagging act. A willing victim, Bill. And the one man could have nipped out of a back window just before I arrived.'

'Well, well,' Beresford said heavily.

'The more I thought about it the more it seemed to me that Eileen had been let off very lightly—as lightly as if she had helped,' Dawlish went on. 'I had other information that you didn't, Bill. I'd talked to and dealt with Eileen Parish. I knew just how hard she seemed to be rooting for Gorman, I knew just how "good" she made herself out to be. The truly good don't rub their righteousness in, they don't even realize that they *are* righteous. The hypocritical keep telling you how good they are, and she certainly did.'

Gorman said as if under his breath: 'God, oh God. And I thought . . .'

He didn't finish.

'Now if Eileen Parish wasn't good, if she wanted Gorman to be suspected and blamed, if she had co-operated with her assailant, she must have a very powerful and compelling motive to want Gorman dead and to hate me. I'd never come across her before, except as someone remotely connected with the case against Gorman, so—why should she hate me enough to want to lay all this on, and make sure that Gorman paid for it?'

No one attempted to answer, except Gorman, who opened his mouth, then shook his head very slowly.

'There was a possible reason,' Dawlish went on. 'I don't yet know whether it's the true one, but I can't see any other. Supposing the boy Max, who was killed running away from me, wasn't her nephew, but her son?' He heard Gorman draw in a hissing breath. 'Supposing that he was her son by Gorman. Supposing Gorman had led their son into the swindle of Mrs. Vaze and so led him to his death—wouldn't she have a motive for hating both Gorman and me?'

Trivett turned to Gorman, who was getting up very slowly as if with an effort, and looked at Dawlish incredulously.

No one spoke, because Gorman was so obviously trying to bring himself to the point of words.

At last, he said huskily.

'You are quite right, Dawlish. It's unbelievable, but you're right in your facts as well as in your reasoning. I hadn't realized what was happening, she'd fooled me, but—Max was our son. My wife and I were—were very deeply in love, but there was a brief affaire between Eileen and me. My wife and I took the child and we brought him up as our own. Until my wife died.' He stared at his sister-in-law, who sat there with her eyes closed and her face as pale as clay. 'Eileen always wanted to marry me, but I could never bring myself to do it. I had no love for her. She was so "good". So "good"?' he echoed, and then threw his hands high into the air and cried: '*So "good", the hypocritical bitch, so "good"!*' Whatever she did she always had a perfect excuse for it, she seduced me because she believed I would get a divorce and marry her—and that she claimed was the will of God!'

Dawlish studied Eileen Parish, and saw that she was looking at Gorman through her lashes. He saw Trivett go to the table where the clock bomb was, and pick it up; this was the one piece of evidence which Trivett could use for a charge immediately; there would be plenty more, but he needed one at once.

'Pat,' Beresford said, and distracted Dawlish's attention for a moment, 'you were much more right than you know. In every way. Thanks. Thanks for——'

Then Eileen Parish leapt up, struck savagely at Gorman and sent him reeling, and sprang towards Trivett, who held the tiny bomb. If it dropped, it would explode in all their faces.

All she wanted was to kill.


### CHAPTER XXIV

### MAN ALIVE

IN THAT awful moment Dawlish thought that the woman would win; saw the glittering light in her light brown eyes, saw the way she struck at Trivett's arm, knew that if she made him drop it, even if he jolted his hand against the table or the wall, it would be enough to set it off. Trivett did not snatch it back, but calmly and coolly swivelled round on the ball of his foot, so that she went by him, pushing him slightly to one side. He did not even lose his balance. Then the other Yard men seized the woman, and she realized that she would never have another chance.

She tightened her lips, and stared fixedly in front of her. She did not say a word when Trivett charged her with attempting to cause grievous bodily harm. She did not look at Dawlish, Beresford or Gorman as she was led out to a police car, and Dawlish had a feeling that she would prob-ably refuse to speak, even in her own defence.

Trivett said, heavily: 'Well, Gorman. You've a lot to thank Dawlish for.'

'Yes.' Gorman said thinly. 'Yes, I can see that. I can see a lot of things clearly now.' He paused, and then went on: 'I can even see that Dawlish does what he believes he ought to do, he . . .' Gorman broke off. 'Dawlish, when I've recovered from this shock, I hope you'll let me come and see you.'

'Whenever you like, and where you like,' Dawlish said. 'Tell me, had you ever given Tenby and Pope cause to want you dead?' He glanced at Trivett. 'That's one of the major questions—why did they talk so freely and name Gorman so eagerly, if it wasn't laid on to fool me?'

'I had worked with Tenby in the old days, I expect you know that,' Gorman answered. 'I put all my money into in-surance, which seemed safe and seemed wise. I didn't trust Tenby, but I trusted the insurance companies and Tenby got his commission, so everything was straight-forward as far as I could see. But now that I know about Eileen . . .' He paused again and closed his eyes; like Beresford, he seemed to have aged but he was still a brown-faced, lean, hard-looking man. 'You see, my will left everything to my sister-in-law, after certain bequests, if my son died before her. It was a lawyer's clause, I did not wish to die intestate, and I have no blood relatives. Eileen would have been wealthy on my death—she had good reason to want me dead, and if you or Beresford killed me . . .' He broke off. 'Dawlish, you will probably think that I am lying. I can only tell you that I am not. My sister-in-law fooled me completely. I thought she was really trying to help me, as the chaplain at Dartmoor and the prison visitors were. Even before I came out, I realized that what had happened was due to—to my own actions. I still hated you. When I saw you here yesterday I could have killed you, but I have since had time to think. I intended to come out of prison and go as straight as I could. I hadn't got to the advanced stage of giving up what money I'd made, but I was what you call reformed. And I was lunatic enough to think that Tenby and Pope between them would be satisfied with a commission for handling my money when I was in Dartmoor. It's obvious now that Eileen knew about the endowments, and that Pope and Tenby had not only hatred of you, Dawlish, but a cut in my money if they helped Eileen.'

140

'That adds up,' Dawlish agreed, and after a few moments' thought, he glanced at Trivett. 'As a matter of fact, Bill, there was another pointer away from Gorman. Tenby said that Gorman had assigned certain endowments to him and Pope, but he could hardly have done from prison. That had the ring of the hurried explanation with a big hole in it. Gorman gives us the answer—Tenby and Pope would have got their money from Eileen Parish.' He paused for a long time, before adding. 'Anyhow, we will talk later.'

'Trivett, if there is any information I can give you to clear up this and any other crimes, I will do so,' Gorman said. 'But as I stand here, I don't know as much about this affair as you and Dawlish.'

'I see,' said Trivett, non-committally.

'I hope that's true,' Dawlish said, and went on: 'Our Eileen really knew how to hate, didn't she? She meant to blow the lot of us up, she was so sure she always held an ace. She even lied about the time you were coming here today, Gorman. You can be sure that she expected Beresford and I to go back to the mews and wait for you around half past five or six.'

'Apparently, yes,' Gorman said.

'All right, Gorman,' Trivett put in. 'We won't worry you more than we have to for a few days, and when we start going back over the old jobs, we'll make it as brief as we can.'

'After all,' Dawlish remarked, 'the police don't have to charge you, you've been inside long enough to pay for all the old crimes, and you'll have to live with your conscience.' He looked at Trivett. 'Bill, first I want to know how Tim is, and then I want to see Felicity.'

'Tim should pull through,' Trivett answered. 'He came round enough to ask for you an hour or so ago. Why not get over to the hospital right away, with Ted? I'll send Felicity over to join you.'

'With a bodyguard,' Dawlish said, and grinned. 'No, I forgot, she won't need one now!' He stepped across to Gorman, put his hand out quite casually, said: 'I'm glad it's worked out this way. Believe it or not, I was always desperately sorry about your son. Ted,' he went on, after a pause, 'we're going sick visiting. Come on!'

Half an hour later thay stepped into the large ward where Tim Jeremy lay in a corner bed, with a blood transfusion unit by its side, and blood dripping persistently into his veins. There was an unexpected brightness in his eyes when

141

he saw Dawlish and Beresford, and their expressions must have told him that it was all over. Dawlish turned to the nurse who was sitting by his side, and when she moved round he saw Felicity in a white cap and white smock. Felicity!

'I had to do *some*thing,' she said, before Dawlish smothered her against him.

Beresford watched them with a grim smile etching those lines at his mouth very deeply; but the killer-look had vanished from his eyes.

\* \* \* \* \*

Felicity had to hear it all. . . .

Dawlish told her exactly what he had told Trivett, when they sat that evening in the living-room of the mews flat, tidied up sufficiently for them to live in for a few days—until Jeremy was completely out of danger. Beresford was at Oxford again. The funeral was tomorrow, and at least he would have only his grief for company there, the hatred would be exorcized.

'. . . and there really isn't much more to tell,' Dawlish said. 'The first inclination was to jump at the obvious solution, that Gorman was behind it, but after the first shock, when I began to think again, that began to look less likely.'

'What do you think will happen to Gorman?' asked Felicity. She was sitting in a large armchair, legs tucked beneath her, while the kitchen door was open and they could just hear the spitting of a roast leg of lamb in the oven.

'He'll probably make a statement about the other women he swindled,' Dawlish said, 'and the Yard and the Public Prosecutor will probably decide that as he served seven years for the one job, he wouldn't have got a much longer sentence if all of them had been taken into consideration. There was his rescue of a warder at Dartmoor, too—the first real indication that he had changed his spots. Do you know,' added Dawlish, as if shocked, 'I'd never even thought of that until this moment!'

## LAY HER AMONG THE LILIES BY JAMES HADLEY CHASE

It was odd that a healthy young heiress like Janet Crosby should die of heart failure. Odder still, that on the day she died she sent a note and $500 to Vic Malloy, private investigator, asking him to trace the person who was blackmailing her sister.

Intrigued by the note, Malloy tried to see Maureen Crosby but only got as far as her nurse – a curvaceous blonde with an engaging bedside manner. Next he tried to see Janet's personal maid, but found that somebody else had reached her first and made sure that she wouldn't talk to anyone – ever again . . .

552 09551 6          35p


## I WOULD RATHER STAY POOR BY JAMES HADLEY CHASE

Like most bank managers, Dave Calvin had acquired an irresistible charm that he could switch on whenever he felt the necessity. Underneath it he was cold, calculating, brutal – a perfect murderer . . .

For years he waited – watching an endless stream of money pass through his hands – knowing that a risk was only worth taking if the reward was justified. And a three hundred thousand dollar payroll was justification enough – even for murder . . .

552 09491 9          35p

# A SELECTED LIST OF CRIME STORIES FOR YOUR READING PLEASURE